Though scattered by years and tears, they share mile-deep roots in one Wyoming ranch—and a singular talent for lassoing the unlikeliest hearts!

"Evie and I are both a little bit nuts about you,"

Bax said in a soft voice.

Carly realized only then that his hands were no longer massaging her foot, but caressing it....

Bax held her eyes with his, and even if Carly had wanted to break away she didn't think she could have. Something about the depth of his gaze kept her hypnotized, enthralled, enchanted.

Why did he have to be so great looking? she wondered. So great smelling? So great all around...?

He reached one hand around to the back of her neck to guide her forward, nearer to him, as he leaned to the side to meet her.

There was no question that he was going to kiss her, and Carly's pulse went into overdrive, beating hard and fast with anticipation. With excitement. With wanting...

Dear Reader,

With spring just around the corner, Silhouette's yearlong 20th Anniversary celebration marches on as we continue to bring you the best and brightest stars and the most compelling stories ever in Special Edition!

Top author Sherryl Woods kicks off the month with *Dylan and the Baby Doctor,* a riveting secret baby story in the next installment of AND BABY MAKES THREE: THE DELACOURTS OF TEXAS.

From beloved author Marie Ferrarella, you'll love *Found: His Perfect Wife,* an emotional story in which a man loses his memory and gains a temporary spouse.... And reader favorite Victoria Pade continues her popular cowboy series A RANCHING FAMILY with *Cowboy's Caress,* a heartwarming story about a woman who's ready to travel the world—until love comes to town!

Millionaire's Instant Baby is rising star Allison Leigh's must-read contribution to the series SO MANY BABIES. In this provocative story, a dashing tycoon gets more than he bargained for when he hires a single mom as his pretend wife in order to close a business deal.

THE BLACKWELL BROTHERS continue to capture hearts in the next book of Sharon De Vita's cross-line series. In *The Marriage Promise,* a Blackwell brother is determined to woo and win the forbidden love of a beautiful Amish virgin. And you won't want to miss *Good Morning, Stranger,* Laurie Campbell's dramatically poignant story about a woman, a child and a handsome, mysterious stranger who uncover secrets that bring together a meant-to-be family.

It's a month chock-full of great reading and terrific variety, and we hope you enjoy all the stories!

All the best,
Karen Taylor Richman
Senior Editor

Please address questions and book requests to:
Silhouette Reader Service
U.S.: 3010 Walden Ave., P.O. Box 1325, Buffalo, NY 14269
Canadian: P.O. Box 609, Fort Erie, Ont. L2A 5X3

VICTORIA PADE

COWBOY'S CARESS

Published by Silhouette Books

America's Publisher of Contemporary Romance

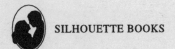

SILHOUETTE BOOKS

ISBN 0-373-24311-1

COWBOY'S CARESS

Copyright © 2000 by Victoria Pade

All rights reserved. Except for use in any review, the reproduction
or utilization of this work in whole or in part in any form by any
electronic, mechanical or other means, now known or hereafter
invented, including xerography, photocopying and recording, or in
any information storage or retrieval system, is forbidden without
the written permission of the editorial office, Silhouette Books,
300 East 42nd Street, New York, NY 10017 U.S.A.

All characters in this book have no existence outside the imagination of
the author and have no relation whatsoever to anyone bearing the same
name or names. They are not even distantly inspired by any individual
known or unknown to the author, and all incidents are pure invention.

This edition published by arrangement with Harlequin Books S.A.

® and TM are trademarks of Harlequin Books S.A., used under license.
Trademarks indicated with ® are registered in the United States Patent
and Trademark Office, the Canadian Trade Marks Office and in other
countries.

Visit us at www.romance.net

Printed in U.S.A.

VICTORIA PADE

is a bestselling author of both historical and contemporary romance fiction, and mother of two energetic daughters, Cori and Erin. Although she enjoys her chosen career as a novelist, she occasionally laments that she has never traveled farther from her Colorado home than Disneyland, instead spending all her spare time plugging away at her computer. She takes breaks from writing by indulging in her favorite hobby—eating chocolate.

IT'S OUR 20ᵗʰ ANNIVERSARY!
We'll be celebrating all year, continuing with these fabulous titles, on sale in March 2000.

Chapter One

"What's that saying? Life is what happens when you have other plans? I guess that applies to you, Carly."

"No doubt about it," Carly Winters agreed from the back seat of her best friend's car where she sat sideways so her foot could be elevated.

But Deana's comment from behind the wheel was a whole lot more lighthearted than Carly's dejected confirmation. Deana had never been happy about Carly's plans to travel so any interference was welcome to her.

"This hasn't canceled my trip, though. It's just postponed it a little," Carly felt inclined to clarify so her friend didn't think otherwise. "The doctors at the emergency room said I'd be as good as new in a few weeks. And then I'm off like a rocket.''

Deana didn't say anything to that. She just turned up the radio and made it seem as if she were paying attention to her driving, as if she had confidence in more of life happening to thwart Carly's plans.

Carly sighed away the feeling of frustration that those thwarted plans left her with—a feeling she was more familiar with than she wanted to be—and laid her head against the seat.

The sun was just rising on the June day she'd been certain would finally be her swan song to Elk Creek, the small Wyoming town where she'd been born, raised and lived almost all of her thirty-two years. Most of which she'd spent thinking—dreaming—about being somewhere else.

But she wasn't headed *away* from Elk Creek. She was headed back to it after spending the night in a Cheyenne hospital emergency room, having her ankle X-rayed.

Luckily she hadn't broken any bones. That could have cost her six weeks in a cast. As it was, her ankle was sprained, the tendons and ligaments were torn, but it was wrapped in an Ace bandage and she'd be able to get around on crutches. And even though it hurt like crazy, she was sure it would heal quicker than a broken ankle would have. Which meant all the sooner that she'd be able to go off on her grand adventure.

Better late than never.

She still couldn't believe it had happened, though. At her going-away party, no less.

The whole thing had been a comedy of errors. There she was, saying goodbye to friends, neighbors and relatives, ready to go home to bed for the last time in Elk Creek, when her sister, Hope, had gone into sudden, hard labor. Their mother had gotten so flustered that in her hurry to reach Hope she'd caught her heel in the hem of her dress. Carly had seen her mother's predicament, dived to catch her and fallen herself, twisting her own ankle to an unhealthy angle while her mother had barely stumbled.

The end result was that Hope had been taken to the medical facility where Tallie Shanahan—the town nurse and midwife—had delivered a healthy baby boy to go with Hope's other three sons, and Deana had taken Carly to the hospital in Cheyenne. Not only had Tallie had her hands full, but she'd been afraid the ankle was broken, requiring the care of a physician—a commodity Elk Creek had been without for some time.

"Maybe this is a sign that you shouldn't go," Deana said from the front seat over the music, letting Carly know her friend was still thinking about her leaving even if Deana tried not to show it.

"It's just a minor setback," Carly countered.

And she meant it, too.

Because nothing—*nothing*—was going to keep her from doing what she'd wanted to do her whole life. Well, since she was seven anyway and her great-aunt Laddy had paid her family a visit and brought photographs of Laddy's travels all over the world.

Carly had studied those pictures until they were

burned into her brain, daydreaming over them, wishing she was seeing the sights in person. Somehow, from that day on, Elk Creek had seemed like small potatoes on the banquet table of the world. And she'd made it her goal to get out into that world and feast on it all herself.

Not that that goal had been easy to reach or it wouldn't have taken her so long to get to it.

First, there had been getting her teaching degree in the nearest college where she and Deana could attend economically by staying with Deana's aunt during the process. Once that was accomplished, Carly had returned to Elk Creek to work and save her traveling money. And then, of course, there had been her involvement with Jeremy and the wrench he'd thrown into the works the past few years.

But now all of that was behind her. She'd saved enough money to last a year or maybe more if she was careful. She'd taken a leave of absence from her job. And if she could ever actually manage to get out of Elk Creek, she was going to see everything she'd ever wanted to see and then pick her favorite city to live in. Maybe not forever, but for long enough to give herself a taste of life outside the confines of her small hometown.

She was going to be a cosmopolitan woman.

By hook or by crook.

Even if it killed her.

"It's not as if I'm moving away permanently," she said with a low concentration of conviction, but wanting to console Deana nonetheless. "I just want to see some things. Do some things. Meet some new people. Live outside the fishbowl for a while. Who knows? A little time away and I'll probably get homesick and come back. That's why I only leased my house and why I didn't out-and-out quit my job.''

''You won't be back if the grass is as green as you think it is on the other side of the fence.''

''Well, even if it is—and it probably isn't—you know it won't make any difference between you and me. We'll still talk all the time, and we can write letters and E-mails and there's nothing in Elk Creek to stop you from coming to wherever I am.''

''It won't be the same as living next door the way we always have.''

Carly knew that was true. She also knew she was going to miss Deana and the way things had been since Deana's family had moved into the house right beside her own when they were both four years old. They'd been together through everything from first kisses to burying their fathers within three months of each other.

Carly's leaving would mean no more seeing each other every day, sharing every detail of their lives. No more late-night binges on ice cream when one or the other of them couldn't sleep and they padded across the lawn in pajamas and bare feet. No more consoling each other at the end of a bad date. No more double dates—good or bad. No more filling each other's lonely hours with company. No more shared bowls of popcorn over tear-jerker movies on videotape to occupy empty Saturday nights. No more impromptu shopping trips or makeover sessions. No more battening down the hatches together in snowstorms. No more working together. No more just being there for each other when either of them needed it for any reason.

But Carly didn't want to think about the downside of leaving town. Instead, she did what she'd been doing to keep herself from dwelling on it since she'd finally decided to do this two months ago: she thought about San Francisco and New York. About seeing Vermont in autumn splendor. About the Alaskan wilderness. About Hawaiian beaches. About London and Paris and Rome and Brussels and Athens and Vienna and Madrid.

About how much she'd always wanted to see it all for herself...

"I still wish you'd come with me," Carly said because that was true, too. She'd tried as long as she'd known Deana to infuse her friend with her own enthusiasm for seeing the world. Short of meeting the man of her dreams on the Orient Express in the middle of her travels, the only other thing that would make the trip perfect would be if Deana had the same wanderlust and they could do it together.

But Carly could see Deana shaking her head even now.

"There isn't anything I want that isn't in Elk Creek."

"Mr. Right," Carly reminded.

"He'll show up one of these days," Deana said with certainty. "And when he does, I don't want to be somewhere else looking at bridges or mountains or leaves or churches or ruins or pyramids."

For as much as they were like two peas in a pod, this was the one area where they differed—Deana was a hometown girl through and through.

And Carly wasn't.

Or at least Carly didn't want to be.

They headed into Elk Creek without fanfare just then. The small enclave's main street—Center Street—was still deserted as Deana drove all the way to where it circled the town square. She turned at the corner taken up by the old Molner Mansion that had been converted into the local medical facility and stopped at the first house behind it. Carly's house. The house her mother had left to her after her father's death, when her mother had decided to move in with Carly's two maiden aunts.

It was a moderate-size yellow clapboard farmhouse with a big front porch, a second level slightly smaller than the lower and a man and a little girl at the oval-glassed front door.

"Looks like you have company," Deana observed as she drove around the station wagon parked at the curb and pulled into the driveway.

"He's not supposed to be here until the middle of the morning," Carly groaned.

"Apparently he arrived ahead of schedule."

"And I'll bet I'm a mess."

Deana reached over and flipped down the visor on the passenger's side so Carly could get a glimpse of herself.

Carly sat up straighter and saw the unruly ends of her straight, shoulder-length auburn hair sticking up every which way at her crown. To get it out of her face she'd twisted it into a knot at the back of her head and jammed a pencil through it.

The blush she'd applied for the party was a thing of the past, although luckily her skin had retained enough color of its own not to leave her looking sickly. Her mauve lipstick was history, too. Her mascara was still in place on longish lashes over topaz-colored eyes, but on the whole she knew she was the worse for wear.

"Not much I can do about it now," she muttered to her reflection as Deana put the idling car in park and got out.

"If you need Carly Winters, I have her right here," Deana called to the people on the porch. "Just give her a minute."

Then Deana opened the rear door and went around to the trunk for Carly's crutches while Carly slid to the end of the seat to wait for them.

"Hi," she said feebly to her guests.

Both the man and the little girl, who looked to be about five or six, had moved from the door to stand at the railing that edged the porch with turned spindles.

The man raised one large hand to acknowledge her greeting.

"Wow," Deana said under her breath as she returned with the crutches, nodding over her shoulder only enough to let Carly know the exclamation was a commentary on the man himself.

As if Carly wouldn't have guessed.

He was tall, no less than six-two, and he looked

much more like a muscled, ranch-rugged cowboy than the town's new doctor she assumed him to be.

His hair was a pale, golden brown he wore short all over. His face had the distinctive McDermot lean angles and rawboned beauty Carly knew only too well since his brothers were residents of Elk Creek. His nose was long and thin and perfectly sculpted. His jaw was square and strong. And his lips were thin, kind and slightly sardonic all at once, not to mention way, way more sexy than Carly wanted to notice.

"Need some help?" he asked when he noticed Carly's dilemma, coming off the porch on long, thick legs that were bowed just enough to look as if they'd spent more time straddling a saddle than standing at an examining table.

He wore faded jeans that rode low on narrow hips, and a plain white T-shirt that stretched tight across broad shoulders, powerful pectorals and bulging biceps that made Carly's stomach do a little flip-flop when she got a closer glimpse of them as he joined her and Deana.

"I think I can manage," Carly said, trying to remember what she'd been taught at the hospital about maneuvering the crutches when her brain was really in a haze due to the man's head-to-toe staggeringly masculine glory.

"You must be Baxter McDermot," she said feebly on her way onto the crutches.

"Bax," he amended.

"*Doctor* McDermot," Deana said with a hint of

flirting in her tone that, for some reason, rubbed Carly wrong.

In spite of it she said, "I'm Carly Winters and this is Deana Carlson."

"I apologize for showing up so early," he said after a confirming nod of his handsome head. "We were in a motel for the night with World War III going on in the room next to us. We finally gave up tryin' to sleep and figured we might as well finish the trip and catch a few winks when we got here."

"Sure. Of course. There's just been a little setback on this end," Carly said, leaning her weight on the crutches and honing in on gorgeous sea-foam green eyes that stamped him a McDermot without a doubt.

"You aren't leaving town and don't want to hand your house over to us," he guessed with a glance down at her bandaged ankle.

"I'm afraid I had an accident last night and I'm going to have to put off leaving until I'm healed up."

"It's okay. We can stay out at the ranch," he offered congenially.

It might have been better if he'd been nasty about it. If he'd reminded her that they had a contract in the form of the lease that guaranteed she would turn the house over to him today.

Instead, he couldn't have been nicer about it, offering to go to the ranch he and his brothers and sister now owned after having taken it over from their grandfather.

The trouble was, Carly knew that wasn't what he

wanted to do or he wouldn't have rented her house in the first place. He'd arranged for the lease because he'd wanted to be closer to the medical facility where he would work—one of the same purposes the house had served for her father when he'd been the town doctor. And there was Bax McDermot's daughter, too. He was determined to be near her so he'd be available to her during the daytime.

Carly knew all this because the real estate agent who had arranged the rental agreement had explained it to her. And now she felt bad that her change of plans had complicated his. She didn't have to be told that if he had to stay out at the McDermot ranch, he'd be pulled in two directions. Not to mention that he wouldn't have this precious time before he actually began seeing patients to get himself and his daughter settled into the house.

He was being such a good sport about it, it just made her feel all the more guilty.

"Listen," she said. "A deal is a deal and according to ours the house is yours as of today. There's a guest cottage just behind it that my dad sometimes used as a makeshift hospital. I could stay there until I'm healed enough to leave and you can have the house. It'll just mean sharing the kitchen, but it will also give me a chance to show you around properly and teach you the workings of the place."

"I don't want to put you out. Maybe I could take the cottage," he offered.

"It's only big enough for one. Besides, I don't mind. It'll actually be easier for me to get around without having to use the stairs in the main house.

And it will only be for a little while. As soon as I'm back on two feet I'm leaving. But in the meantime, things won't have to be messed up for you.''

He seemed to study her for a sign that she meant what she said.

She aided the cause by adding, ''Really, I don't mind.''

He finally conceded. ''If you're sure…''

''I am.''

''Okay, then. Great,'' he agreed with a slight shrug of broad shoulders and a smile that put dimples in both cheeks and made Carly's head go light.

Not that her reaction had anything to do with him, she told herself in a hurry. She was just overly tired.

''Do you need me?'' Deana asked.

Only in that moment did Carly remember her friend, and she was ashamed of herself for having been so focused on Bax McDermot that she'd forgotten her.

''I'm fine,'' Carly assured too effusively. ''Thanks for taking me to Cheyenne and everything else, Dee.''

''You'd do the same for me. At least if you were around,'' her friend said pointedly. ''I'll check with you this afternoon. If you need me in the meantime, just holler.''

''Thanks,'' Carly repeated as Deana closed the rear car door then got behind the wheel.

''Nice to meet you,'' the new doctor said to Deana.

''You, too,'' Deana answered just before she

backed out of Carly's driveway only to pull into the one next door.

"Short trip," Bax McDermot observed with a laugh as he watched the move.

Annoyance struck Carly for the second time as she caught sight of the big man's gaze following her friend.

She really did need sleep, she decided. Lack of it was making her cranky.

"We might as well go in," she urged, taking her first steps on the crutches.

But heading across the lawn was a tactical error, and by the third uncoordinated three-legged hobble she set one of the crutches in a hole and everything went into a careen.

Bax McDermot lunged for her, catching her just short of falling with both of those big hands on her waist.

"Steady," he advised.

But even though he'd accomplished just that, something about the warm feel of his hands sent things inside her reeling.

"Sorry," she apologized, feeling like an idiot. "I haven't had much practice on these things."

"They work better on solid surfaces."

Before she had any inkling of what he was going to do, he scooped her up into his arms and carried her to the porch on long, sturdy strides, setting her down near one of the posts so she could hang on to it for balance.

The whole trip took only a few seconds and yet

that close contact had knocked her for even more of a loop.

So much so that it took her a moment of hard work to regain herself and realize he was introducing his daughter.

"This is Evie Lee."

"Evie Lee Lewis," the little girl corrected.

"Evie Lee McDermot is what's on her birth certificate," Bax explained. "She tacked on the Lewis herself a few months ago. I can't tell you why or where she got it."

"Everybody should have three first names," Evie Lee added. "To tell them apart from everybody else."

"Makes sense to me," Carly agreed, seizing the distraction of the child.

"Why don't you run and get the crutches?" Bax suggested to his daughter.

Evie Lee did just that, dragging them behind her on her return trip.

She was a tiny little thing with blond hair and a face that was the impish image of her father's, complete with beautiful green eyes that Carly knew would break some hearts down the line.

She thanked Evie Lee when she took the crutches from her and was all too aware of Evie Lee's father keeping his hands at the ready to catch her again when she turned and made her way to the front door on them.

"It isn't locked," she informed him when they'd reached it and he seemed to be waiting for her to produce a key. "No reason to lock doors in Elk

Creek. It isn't a high-crime area, so nobody bothers for the most part.''

"Nice," he commented as he opened the old-fashioned screen and then the heavy oak panel with the leaded glass oval in its center.

Carly hobbled through ahead of him, stopping in the entryway at the foot of the stairs that led to the upper level. "We're all too tired for the tour, so I'll just give you directions, if that's okay."

"Fine."

"The master bedroom is the first one at the top of the steps. I thought Evie Lee might like the one beside it. That was my sister's and it's still all done up for a little girl. I got them both ready for you yesterday, so there's clean sheets on the beds and empty drawers for your things. The bathroom is down the hall a ways, along with the linen closet and the other bedrooms. Down here, you can see the kitchen at the end of this hall. That's the living room—" she nodded over her right shoulder toward the room they could see from where they all stood "—and the dining room is beyond it, connected to the kitchen. There's another bathroom and the den that you get to from under the stairs."

"All we really need for right now are beds."

"Me, too. The cottage is just across the back patio. That's where I'll be if you need me," she said, pivoting on the crutches to face that direction.

"Can I help you get there?" he asked.

"No. I'm fine. Really," she insisted, adding, "Sleep well," just before heading down the hall on her own.

She could feel him watching her the whole way, and she was glad when she finally got far enough into the kitchen to be out of his line of vision.

But somehow that didn't take away the lingering sense of those eyes on her and the inexplicable feeling of heat that they'd caused.

All part of the weird side effects of a sleepless night, she told herself.

But still she hoped she hadn't made a mistake in keeping her agreement to let Bax McDermot move in before she'd actually moved out.

Because sleep-deprived or not, something inside her was sitting up and taking notice of too many things about the man.

And that didn't have any place at all in her plans.

Chapter Two

For a split second when Bax first woke up he thought he was back in the days of his residency when it wasn't unusual to work a twenty-four-hour shift and catch forty winks in any empty bed he could find, at any time of day he could manage it.

Then he remembered that he was long past that particular portion of his life and he searched his memory until he recalled that he was in Elk Creek, Wyoming, in the bed in one of the rooms in the house he'd rented.

Carly Winters's house.

A wave of satisfaction washed through him.

He was just so damn glad to be out of the city.

He was a small-town boy at heart. Always had

been. Except that the small town he'd grown up in had been in Texas rather than in Wyoming.

It had been exciting to leave that small town and go to medical school, exciting to practice medicine in the hub of that same university since then. But he'd had a change of heart over the past couple of years. A change of heart that had made him want all he'd left behind. For himself. And for Evie Lee. Especially for Evie Lee.

He felt as if his daughter had gotten short shrift in the parent department so far in her young life. His wife had died on the delivery table, leaving Evie Lee semiorphaned right from the get-go. And Bax knew he hadn't been the best of dads since then.

He'd thrown himself into his work to escape a grief that had seemed unbearable any other way, building up one of the largest medical practices in Denver. That had meant sixty- and seventy-hour workweeks, being on call most nights and weekends, and generally putting fatherhood second.

It had meant leaving Evie Lee in the care of a string of live-in nannies. Not all of whom had treated her well.

He wasn't proud of any of that.

But he was going to rectify it.

Here and now, he thought as he opened his eyes to glance at the clock on the bedside table.

Three o'clock on a Sunday afternoon and a new life had begun for both him and Evie Lee. He'd make sure of it.

Bax yawned, stretched, then clasped his hands behind his head and had a look around the room that had been predesignated his.

The bed was a fair-size four-poster. At the foot of it was a television on a stand against the facing wall. A tall, five-drawer dresser was to the right of the bed. And a door that no doubt led to a closet was to the left.

The whole room was painted a serene shade of beige, with the woodworking all stained oak. Crisp tieback white curtains bordered the two large windows on either side of the television, with scalloped shades pulled down to the sills of both.

The room was comfortable. Functional. Charmingly old-fashioned.

He liked it.

And he wondered if this had been Carly Winters's own room.

Probably not, he decided. It didn't smell the way she did.

Not that it smelled anything but clean. But he sort of wished it had that faintly lingering scent of honey and almonds that he'd caught a whiff of when he'd carried her to the porch. It was a nice smell.

A nice smell to go with a nice-looking lady, he thought.

Sure, she'd shown the wear and tear of a long night in an emergency room. But despite that, she was still a head-turner.

Besides smelling great, her hair was so smooth and silky and shiny, it had made him want to yank that pencil out of it and watch the tresses drift like layers of silk down around her face.

A face that glowed with flawless, satiny skin.

She had a rosebud of a mouth that was pink and perfect and much too appealing even without lipstick. She also had a cute, perky nose that was dotted with only a few pale freckles he wouldn't have noticed if he hadn't been so close.

Artfully arched eyebrows and long, thick lashes accentuated stunning, unusual eyes, too. Brown eyes, but shot through with golden streaks that made them the color of topaz. Sparkling topaz.

Her body hadn't been anything to ignore, either. She was on the small side, weighing next to nothing when he'd lifted her. But petite stature or not, when she'd put her arm around his shoulder to help bear some of the burden, he'd felt a more than adequate breast press enticingly into his shoulder.

Oh yeah, it was all nice. Very nice…

And strange that he should remember everything about her so vividly.

Particularly when the other woman he'd met that morning was just a vague blur in his mind. He wasn't even sure he'd recognize the other woman again if he met her on the street, and for the life of him he couldn't recall her name.

Yet every detail of Carly Winters was right there in his mind's eye.

Making him stare up at the ceiling with a smile on his face…

Cut it out, he told himself.

But that was easier said than done.

In fact, it was damn difficult to get her out of his thoughts, he discovered when he tried.

Maybe it was just that he was in her house, in a room that might have been hers. In a bed she might have slept in...

The idea of that stirred even more uninvited responses inside him, and he wondered where the hell it was all coming from.

But wherever this reaction was coming from, he put a concerted effort into chasing it away, reminding himself that he hadn't moved to Elk Creek to think...or feel...things like he was thinking and feeling at that moment. It just wasn't in his game plan.

He'd come to the small town to concentrate on practicing medicine and to raise his daughter hands-on, full-time, which was why it had been so important to live a stone's throw from where he worked. And he wasn't interested in trying to add a woman to the picture. He'd already made that mistake once, and he wasn't going to make it again.

But not even the reminder of his second marriage, which was the worst thing he'd ever done in his life and in Evie Lee's, not even his determination to conquer those thoughts of Carly helped to get the image of her out of his head. Or stopped those stirred-up feelings that went with them.

"Must be the house," he muttered, convincing himself that the place was somehow infused with the essence of her, and that was why he couldn't stop thinking about her, remembering how she'd looked, smelled, felt in his arms.

But as soon as she was gone and he and Evie Lee had settled in and taken over the place, all that would be different. The house would be theirs and Carly Winters would only be a faint memory.

He was sure of it.

He just wondered how long it would take for her to be well enough to leave.

And that was when he realized he hadn't even asked what was wrong with her or what kind of an accident she'd had.

"Some good doctor you are," he chastised himself.

But he *was* a good doctor. Ordinarily. In fact, he'd been named Doctor of the Year for the past four years running. Yet meeting Carly Winters had thrown him off-kilter.

Oh yeah, something very strange was going on, all right.

But strange or not, topaz eyes or not, honey-scented hair or not, it didn't matter. Before long Carly Winters would be gone and he was going to be the best damn doctor Elk Creek had ever had. And, more importantly, the best damn dad Evie Lee could possibly have.

And that was that.

Except that even as he sat up and swung his legs over the edge of the mattress his first thought was whether Carly was up and about yet.

And if their paths might cross again anytime soon...

Carly might have slept longer if not for the quiet humming that was coming from beside her bed.

There was no real tune to it and it was terribly

off-key, so she knew from the start that it wasn't coming from the clock radio on the nightstand. And since no one had any reason to be in the cottage at all, let alone while she slept, the sound brought her abruptly awake.

Her eyes opened to the sight of the youngest of her new tenants sitting patiently on the dated, barrel-backed chair that was against the wall to the left of the bed, facing it.

Evie Lee was dressed just as she'd been when Carly had first seen her on the porch—short pink overalls and a white T-shirt dotted with rosebuds. But her wavy blond hair was matted and standing up on one side as if that were the side she'd slept on and hadn't bothered to brush or comb since getting up.

If Carly had to bet on it, she'd wager that Evie Lee had woken up and come exploring without her father's knowledge. He was probably still asleep. Or at least thought his daughter was.

"Hi," the little girl said when she saw Carly's eyes open.

"Hi."

"I got tired of sleepin' and I came to visit you. Is that okay?"

"You can visit me any time at all," Carly answered.

Evie Lee glanced around. "I like this place. It's like a big playhouse."

That was true enough. The cottage was one large room—with the exception of a separate bathroom. Only the furniture divided the open space into sections. A double bed, the antique oak nightstand and the visitor's chair Evie Lee was occupying made up the bedroom. A round, pedestaled café table with two cane-backed chairs and a wet bar were the dining area. A pale-blue plaid love seat, matching overstuffed chair and a television comprised the living room, although the TV was positioned so that it could be seen from anywhere in the room.

The cottage had a history as a guest house and also as a sometimes hospital room where her father had put up patients he'd wanted to keep a close eye on.

It was pleasant and airy, though, with off-white walls of painted paneling and ruffled curtains on the windows to give it a homey atmosphere.

"I don't remember your name," the little girl said bluntly.

"Carly."

"Is that what I can call you, or do I have to call you Miss or something like at school?"

"You can call me Carly."

"You can call me Evie Lee Lewis."

"Thank you," Carly said with a smile, sitting up in bed and bracing her back against the headboard. "Have you been to school yet?" she asked the little girl.

"I went to kindergarten before the summer and when the summer is over and it's schooltime again I'll be in the first grade. You go all day long in that grade. I hope I like it. I hope it's not too much stressful. Alisha had a lot of stressfuls and then she'd go to bed and I wouldn't want to have to go to first grade and then have to go to bed.''

"Alisha?" Carly repeated, her interest sparked at the mention of a woman's name.

"Alisha was my sort-of mom for a while but she didn't like me. She liked my daddy. But she didn't like me. She said I was a bad kid and that I was a stressful and a pest and a pain-in-the—''

"Where did she go?"

"Away. My daddy sent her away because she locked me in the closet because I was naughty one day and I put on her shoes and messed up some of her lipsticks."

The thought of putting this little girl or any other child in a closet raised Carly's hackles. "Sounds like your daddy did the right thing by sending her away."

"He was really mad."

"Good for him. He should have been."

"How did you hurt yourself?"

"I fell and sprained my ankle."

"I got a bad scratch on my elbow. See?" Evie Lee displayed the underside of her elbow. "I got it on Mikey Stravoni's slide and then I got a scab but I picked at it till it comed off and then it bleeded all over the place and my daddy said 'I told you not to pick off that scab' because he's a doctor."

Carly laughed at the lowered-voice imitation, enjoying the child who looked so much like her father that staring at her conjured flashes of the man himself in Carly's mind's eye. Flashes that left her with more eagerness to see him again than she wanted to acknowledge.

"Does your ankle hurt?" Evie Lee asked.

"A little."

"Sometimes if you pinch yourself really hard somewhere else you'll forget about it."

"I'll remember that."

"Could I play with your crutches when you don't need 'em?"

"Sure, but they'll be awfully big for you."

"You have pretty eyes."

"So do you."

"I have pretty hair, too," Evie Lee said matter-of-factly. "Will you show me how to put a pencil in it?"

"I will if you want me to. But we could probably put something prettier than a pencil in it."

"Okay," Evie Lee said with enthusiasm, her pale eyebrows taking flight with the anticipation. "My daddy is no good at hair combing. He says he could do surgery better. Do you have any l'il kids?"

"I'm afraid not. I'm not married."

"Me, neither. My daddy isn't neither, too. Are there any l'il kids around here to play with?"

Carly eased herself to the edge of the bed, letting both feet dangle over the side to test how her ankle felt when it wasn't propped up. It hurt more, but it wasn't unbearable.

"There's a little girl up the street," she answered.

"How old is she?"

"I think she's six."

"That's good. That's how old I am—six. I just

turned it and I got Angel Barbie for my birthday because she's the prettiest one.''

"You'll have to show her to me."

"I could go get her now."

"I think we'll have to do that later. My sister is at the medical building where your daddy will be working. She just had a baby last night and I want to go over and see how she is."

"What kind of baby?"

"A boy."

"Can I come with you?"

Carly laughed again, not minding the little girl's chattiness or persistence. "It's okay with me if it's okay with your dad. But we can't go without checking with him first."

Evie Lee hopped out of the chair. "I'll go ask him right now."

"I want to clean up and then I'll come across to the house to check with him."

"I'll clean up, too," Evie Lee said as if she liked the idea.

The child ran for the door, opened it and turned back to Carly. "See ya."

"See ya," Carly answered.

And out went Evie Lee.

Since Carly wasn't too sure whether or not the little girl might return within minutes—alone or with her father—she wasted no time getting to her crutches and heading for the bathroom.

But on the way she realized she was wearing only her slip, that the dress she'd had on the night before was tossed over the back of the love seat, and that she hadn't brought any of her things with her from the house.

That meant she couldn't take the fast shower she had in mind or so much as run a comb through her hair or brush her teeth or fix her face or change her clothes.

It also meant that if Bax McDermot was up and about, she was going to have to meet him looking even worse than she had the first time.

Not a proposition she relished.

But what was she going to do? She was in the cottage and everything she needed was in the house. She didn't have any choice.

Her only hope was that he was still asleep and she could slip in and out before he woke up.

With that in mind, she put her dress back on over her slip and made her way out of the cottage.

The cottage was separated from the main house by only an eight-foot, brick-paved breezeway. The breezeway was covered on top but open on either side so it could be used as a patio in good weather. There was a cedar wood bench seat along one side, but Carly had left the rest of the patio furniture—chairs and small tables—in the garage so far this season. Minus the clutter of it, she maneuvered herself and the crutches across the breezeway without impediment.

When she reached the back door, she peeked in the window that filled the top half of it and spotted Evie Lee alone in the kitchen, standing on a ladder-backed chair to get herself a glass of water.

Carly knocked on the door to draw the child's

attention and then opened it enough to poke her head in. "Is your dad around?"

"He's in the shower so I didn't ask him yet about going with you. But he'll be out in a little bit."

Carly didn't want to think about Bax being in her shower. *Naked* in her shower...

"I need to get up to my room. All my things are still in it."

Evie Lee jumped down from the chair as if it were a tall cliff. "Okay. Come on."

Carly pushed the door open wide with the end of one crutch and got herself through it. But as she did, it occurred to her that if she didn't let the new doctor know she was coming inside, she was liable to bump into him accidentally. As he left the bathroom after his shower. Maybe not dressed...

And while that possibility erupted some wild goose bumps on the surface of her skin, she knew she couldn't let it happen.

"I think it might be a good idea for you to go up and warn him I'm here."

"It's all right. He's always in the shower for a looong time. Come on," Evie Lee encouraged with a flapping wave of her hand, shooting off ahead of Carly.

Carly didn't seem to have a choice but to follow, wishing the whole way that she could just send Evie Lee to get what she needed.

But most everything was packed and Carly had closed the suitcases to make sure she could. Evie Lee was too small to deal with what it would involve to get into them.

The stairs to the upper level presented a problem and after several attempts with the crutches, Carly conceded that she needed help.

Since Evie Lee was already on the landing at the top, Carly said, "I'm going to need you to carry the crutches up for me. But why don't you let your dad know I'm coming first."

Evie Lee shrugged and did her little-girl-happy-dance until she was out of sight.

Carly heard her holler through the door to her father that Carly was there, but no answer came in response.

"He can't hear me," Evie Lee said a moment later, at the top of the steps again. "It'll be all right. I told you, he'll be in there for a really, really long time."

The prospect of standing there waiting for that really, really long time was not appealing. Especially when the alternative was that Carly could get in and out of her room without seeing him at all.

"Okay. Come and get the crutches for me, then."

The child obliged and while Evie Lee dragged them up in front of Carly, Carly used the banister to aid in hopping one step at a time on her good foot.

It was noisy and awkward and Carly kept up a silent chant of *Please don't let him come out of the bathroom, Please don't let him come out of the bathroom,* the whole way.

When both she and Evie Lee had finally made it to the top and Carly was on the crutches again, she realized that sometime during the trip the shower water had stopped running. Not a good sign.

Before she moved from that spot at the top of the stairs, she said, "It sounds like your dad is out of the shower. Knock on the bathroom door and yell in again to let him know I'm out here."

"Okay," the child agreed as if she just didn't understand what the big deal was.

But Evie Lee barely made it to the door when it opened before she had the chance to do or say anything. And out stepped Bax.

It was obvious he was fresh from the shower. His short hair was still damp and all he had on was a pair of faded blue jeans that rode low on his hips. His feet were bare and so was his entire upper body—broad shoulders, big biceps, muscled pectorals, flat belly and all.

And an even worse case of goose bumps sprang to the surface of Carly's skin than the mere thought of the same scenario had caused.

"Whoops," Evie Lee said at the look of surprise on her father's face. "I was just comin' to tell you Carly was out here."

"I'm sorry," Carly was quick to say. Once she could drag her eyes off his chest. "I didn't bring any of my stuff with me to the cottage, and I was trying to get to my room for it now. Evie Lee knocked before and called in to you, but you must not have been able to hear her."

And didn't Carly just want to crawl into a hole rather than face him looking the way she did!

Bax recovered himself and granted her a smile

that made her suddenly feel wobbly on the crutches.
"No problem. Do you want to use the bathroom up
here?"

Hot, steamy air was wafting out into the hallway,
smelling like a far more manly soap than she'd ever
used. The idea of stepping into that was too arousing
to entertain.

"No, I'd rather just take my things down to the
cottage."

"How did you plan to do that?" he asked reasonably.

Only then did it occur to her that he was right.
How was she going to manage suitcases and
crutches, too?

"I guess I hadn't thought it through," she admitted.

"I don't mind if you want to use the bathroom
up here, but if you'd rather not I can carry your
things down to the cottage for you."

She didn't know how he could be so calm and
collected when she felt like a blithering idiot.

But then, he wasn't looking at the magnificent
specimen she was looking at. He was looking at her,
dressed in the same rumpled sundress she'd gone to
her going-away party in, her face unwashed in more
hours than she wanted to think about and her hair
straggling around her ears, weeping for a comb.

"It would be great if you could bring my suitcases down to the cottage," she said when she found
her voice. "There's a full bathroom down there. In
fact, it's better equipped for someone incapacitated

because my dad sometimes had patients stay there. Well, not in the bathroom—I mean, he'd have patients stay in the cottage. But the bathroom has grab bars and a seat in the shower and—''

She stopped herself before she babbled anymore.

''Anyway,'' she said, ''I'd really appreciate it if you could bring my suitcases down. That would be great.''

''Why don't you show me which room is yours and I'll get them,'' he said.

Carly pointed with a nod of her chin to the end of the hall. ''It's that one.''

''Can I go with Carly to visit her sister in the hospital?'' Evie Lee said then.

Carly explained what the child was talking about as she followed Bax into her room.

''So I have two patients already,'' he said as he put Carly's carry-on bag under one arm, picked up the smaller of the other two to tote in one hand and then hoisted the largest in the opposite hand.

''I don't think there were any complications or anything,'' she answered, trying not to watch the flex and swell of his muscles in the process. ''Tallie Shanahan—she's our nurse and midwife—delivered the baby, and when I called from Cheyenne, she said everything was fine. So I don't know if you'd call Hope and the baby your patients.''

''I should still look in on them. How about if we all go together? You can show us the way.''

''Sure. That would be fine,'' Carly said, feeling anything but fine.

She hated that just being near this man could re- duce her to some kind of bumbling schoolgirl.

She took a deep breath to try to get control over herself. "I'd like to shower first, though," she added.

"Need help?"

"No!" she said in too much of a hurry before being sure if he was teasing her, flirting with her, or if he was offering medical aid.

But the glint in his green eyes and the hint-of- the-devil smile that brought out his dimples made her inclined to think he was teasing. And flirting.

"Like I said," she continued, "the shower is equipped for people who aren't at their best. Be- sides, they told me at the hospital that I could un- wrap my ankle to bathe and then just wrap it again, so I shouldn't be too handicapped."

"Did they show you how to wrap it again after- ward?"

"No, but I'm sure it won't be too hard."

"You might be surprised. If you wrap it too loose, it won't do any good and too tight will do damage. Why don't you leave it unwrapped and I'll do that for you before we go over to the hospital? At least I can teach you how to do it right so you can take care of it yourself from here on out."

There was no mistaking his more professional tone.

"Well, okay," Carly agreed without enthusiasm. Somehow just the thought of his touching her—even only her ankle—made flutters of something she didn't understand go off in the pit of her stomach.

"Let's get you back downstairs then," he suggested.

Carly did an ungraceful about-face on the crutches and headed for the stairs again.

At the top of them she hesitated, unsure how best to make the descent.

"You probably ought to go down on your rear end," came the advice from behind her in a deep, baritone voice edged with amusement once more.

There was no way she was going to sit and slide down those stairs while he watched!

Carly ignored his recommendation, handed Evie Lee the crutches again and bounced on her good foot from step to step much the way she'd gone up.

Granted, it wasn't an improvement in the grace or aplomb department, but at least it was quick and didn't involve her rear end.

Once she was at the bottom she held her head high, accepted the crutches from her tiny assistant, and led the way through the house, back to the cottage with Bax and Evie Lee both following behind.

Only when she was in the middle of the cottage again did she turn to find that Bax McDermot was trying to hide a laugh. At her.

"Are you always this headstrong?" he asked.

"I got here, didn't I?"

He just chuckled and raised her bags. "Where shall I put these?"

"Set the big one on the table, the carry-on on one

of the chairs beside it and the smaller bag in the corner,'' she instructed. ''If you wouldn't mind,'' she added to soften the command.

The cottage had never felt as small to Carly as it did then. Bax was a big man and he seemed to fill the space with a heady masculinity that seeped through Carly's pores and made her almost dizzy.

She couldn't keep from watching as he did as she'd told him. Her gaze was glued to his bare back where it widened from his narrow waist to the expanse of his shoulders in smooth-skinned glory. No doctor should have a body like that, she decided. It put too many other men to shame.

And she had to fight the itch in her palms to reach out and run them over the hills and valleys of honed muscle.

Then he turned to face her once more and tearing her eyes off his chest again became a battle she almost lost until she reminded herself that the last thing in the world she wanted was to be attracted to a man right now. Any man.

But it still took a force of will to yank her gaze up to his face.

Too bad that didn't allow her any relief. Because the chiseled planes of his ruggedly perfect features only made her feel dizzy all over again.

''Need me for anything else?'' he asked.

Needs were just what were churning inside her, but none he could meet in front of his daughter.

Or anywhere else, for that matter, without disrupting Carly's plans more than they'd already been disrupted.

And she wasn't going to let that happen.

"No, thanks. But thanks for helping me get my stuff down here."

"How long shall I give you before I come back to wrap your ankle?"

"Half an hour?"

"Perfect."

Yes, he was. Damn him, anyway.

"Come on, Evie, let's do something with your hair," he said to his daughter then.

The little girl skipped out ahead of him, clearly oblivious to her father's effect on Carly. As was Bax, Carly hoped.

But only after they'd both left and closed the door behind them did Carly breathe freely again.

The trouble was, this time she couldn't blame her response to Bax McDermot on lack of sleep. She had to admit that it was purely a reaction to something about the man himself.

But she had too much at stake to let it get beyond goose bumps and weak knees and itchy palms and dizziness and flutters in her stomach. She likened her reaction to sneezing when she got anywhere near ragweed—inevitable, inescapable, and over as soon as she got away from the ragweed or took her antihistamine.

She just needed to get away from Bax McDermot.

Which was exactly what she would be doing in just a few days.

In the meantime, she'd simply have to grit it out and keep reminding herself that she didn't want anything to foul up her plans any more than they already had been.

Because unfortunately she didn't think her antihistamine would be of any help with this particular reaction.

Chapter Three

Carly took the fastest shower of her life. Not an easy task when she had to do it standing on one foot like a flamingo lawn ornament. But there was absolutely, positively no way she was going to come face-to-face with Bax McDermot for the third time without being presentable.

With that in mind—actually with Bax in mind—she gelled her hair to give it body and let it air dry while she slipped into a pair of flowing rayon overalls in a red- and cream-colored batik print over a tight-fitting short-sleeve T-shirt.

She applied just enough blush to give her high cheekbones a healthy glow, mascara enough to accentuate every single eyelash and a pale gloss that guaranteed kissable lips.

Of course that kissable part didn't matter, she assured herself, ignoring a second eruption of those stomach flutters at the thought.

By then her hair was dry, so she brushed it and pulled it to the top of her head in an elastic scrunchee and let the slight bit of natural wave on the ends have its way.

A scant splash of perfume was the final touch. Even though she knew there was no call for it, she couldn't resist. She just rejected any thought that her desire to smell sweet and sexy and alluring had anything to do with the new town doctor.

She was in the midst of stashing the perfume bottle back in her carry-on bag when the knock on the cottage door came.

She took one quick look at herself in the full-length mirror on the bathroom door, approved of the improvement, and called "Come in," in a voice she hardly recognized because it sounded so giddy and unlike her.

Bax only poked his handsome head through the door. "Are you ready for us?"

"Sure," she answered after clearing her throat, this time sounding as calm as if she hadn't just hopped around the place like a rabbit in fast-forward mode.

"You *look* ready," he said, stepping inside and giving her the once-over as he did. Then he dimpled up with an appreciative smile that made her crazed hop worth it.

At least it would have if she'd been admitting to herself that she cared.

Behind him came Evie Lee, closing the door and turning to Carly, too. "Daddy wouldn't put a pencil in my hair," the little girl complained rather than saying hello.

Carly didn't mind the omission. She was grateful for the distraction from Bax's dimples and lowered her gaze to the child.

Evie Lee's hair no longer stood up or was matted on one side. It was combed smooth all over, but merely left to fall loosely around her thin shoulders.

"Could you put the pencil in it now and maybe another time we could use a barrette?" Evie Lee persisted.

Carly looked to Bax for permission. "Do you mind?"

He rolled his eyes, shook his head and answered so slowly it was clear he'd been exasperated with the subject before ever getting to the cottage. "If she wants a pencil in her hair and you're willing to put a pencil in her hair, then be my guest and put a pencil in her hair."

"I'm willing," Carly said with a laugh at his controlled loss of patience.

Since she was near the table and chairs where her suitcases were, she pulled the free chair out from under the table and sat on it.

Both the pencil Carly had used in her own hair earlier and her brush were close at hand so she motioned Evie Lee to stand in front of her.

Evie Lee came on a twirl of delight, stopping with her back to Carly.

It took only a few swipes of the brush to pull the

silky tendrils off the child's neck. Then Carly twisted Evie Lee's hair into a loose knot at the crown and stuck the writing implement through it.

"There you go," Carly said when she'd finished.

Evie Lee ran for the same mirror Carly had used moments before to check her own appearance and preened before it.

"Oh, that's so cute!" the little girl said.

Carly laughed again, enjoying Evie Lee's enthusiasm.

"What do you say?" Bax prompted his daughter.

"Thank you, thank you, thank you!" the child gushed.

Bax sighed out another breath as if he were glad to have that over with and said, "Okay, now for more important things than pencils as hair doohickeys."

That drew Carly's attention back to him.

Until that moment she hadn't noticed he'd brought with him a black medical bag much like the one her father had carried. He set it on the floor by her feet, then hunkered down on his heels in front of her. Opening the bag, he took a fresh bandage from it as Carly hiked up her pant leg just to mid-calf, exposing an ankle swollen to triple normal size and turned a variegated shade of midnight-and-blueberry blue.

"You did a number on this, didn't you?" Bax observed, studying the results of her fall. "So, what was your diagnosis?"

"Sprained ankle with torn ligaments and strained tendons. But no broken bones," Carly recited.

"How did it happen?" he asked, still surveying it with only his eyes.

Carly explained the chain of events that had landed her sprawled on the floor at her going-away party.

"Well, at least you can say it happened in an attempt to do a good deed," Bax said when she'd finished the story, barely suppressing a laugh at her recounting. "Let's get it wrapped again for you. It'll feel better."

And with that he cupped her heel in the palm of his hand and raised it to rest on the thick, hard ledge of his thigh.

There wasn't anything the slightest bit unprofessional or improper or out of the ordinary about what he did. Yet that was all it took for the whole array of sensations to kick in again, adding streaks of lightning to the list as they shot from her ankle all the way up her leg when he began to wrap the bandage expertly around her foot.

No doubt about it, having him touch her was not a good idea.

She didn't know how hands that big could be so warm and gentle when they looked as if they belonged on the reins of a horse instead. But gentle they were. Exquisitely, enticingly gentle.

And worse than all the sensations going through her again was the intense desire to feel the touch of those hands on other places. Much more intimate places...

He was explaining to her how to wrap the bandage, but she only realized it belatedly. When she did, she yanked her thoughts out of the instant reverie his touch had elicited and tried to concentrate so she could perform this task for herself.

"We can soak this a couple of times a day and keep it elevated as much as possible," he was saying. "But mainly with an injury like this you just have to wait it out."

"Too bad. I'd do just about anything to speed up the healing process," she heard herself say all the while she was thinking, *Anything to speed up the healing process and get me out of town and away from everything being near you does to me.*

He didn't seem aware of the internal turmoil he was causing with his ministrations, though, which was one thing to be grateful for, Carly thought. Still, it would have been nice to be able to turn off the turmoil altogether.

When he'd finished with the bandage, her ankle was wrapped perfectly. He lowered her heel to the floor much the way he'd raised it to his thigh before and Carly suffered pangs of disappointment that the whole thing was over even as she silently screamed at herself to stop the insanity that seemed to overcome her every time she was around this guy.

Bax closed the bag and took it with him as he stood. "Done," he announced.

Carly only wished her response to him was done, too.

But even though it wasn't, she pretended it was, got to her good foot and hopped to where her crutches waited against the wall not far away.

"Thanks," she said, not sounding genuinely

grateful and regretting the flippancy in her tone. After all, it wasn't *his* fault she'd turned into a sack of mush over him. He didn't even know what was going on with her. So, feeling guilty, she added, "I really appreciate this."

"Glad to do it," he assured. But as he watched her wiggle around for the right position on the crutches, wobble, then right herself, his expression turned dubious. "Maybe we should drive to the medical center rather than walk," he suggested.

The idea of being in an enclosed car with him was too dangerous at that point. Carly would have crawled to the medical building rather than that.

"It's only across the way. I'd have to walk farther to get out to the car than to get where we're going. There's a path from the backyard over to the Molner Mansion."

"The Molner Mansion?" he repeated as Carly led the way to the door. He still managed to get there enough ahead of her to open it for her.

She explained that the three-story redbrick building had belonged to one of the founding families of Elk Creek and had been donated to the town as the medical building. She also told Bax and Evie Lee that it contained what would be Bax's office, examining rooms, the emergency center, the dental office, outpatient surgery facilities and two rooms that acted as hospital rooms when the necessity arose.

By then they'd reached the mansion and again Bax held the door open for her and Evie Lee to enter before him.

"Do you want a tour of the place?" she offered.

"How about tomorrow? Afternoon naps always leave Evie hungry, so I thought maybe we'd just visit our patients and then go home and I'd whip up some supper for the three of us. Which reminds me, thanks for stocking the refrigerator. That was really thoughtful."

Carly could feel her face flush. Doing a good deed was one thing, but it embarrassed her to have it mentioned.

"It was nothing," she said as she pushed the button for the single elevator that had been installed in the building to accommodate moving patients from one floor to the other.

Carly had ridden the elevator more times than she could begin to count, but never had it seemed so small.

Or smelled so good.

She breathed in the same scent that had come out of the bathroom with Bax when she'd met him in the hall of the main house, enjoying the second helping of it more than she wanted to. She was glad the trip to the second floor was quick.

But she was also slightly disappointed again when it was over and she had to leave the confines that allowed her the heady indulgence.

Maybe the fall that had sprained her ankle had knocked something loose in her brain, she thought, and left her a little nuts.

It didn't take much to tell which room her sister was in because that was where the voices and laughter were coming from when they got off the elevator, so Carly led Bax and Evie Lee there, too.

One step inside the room changed the tone of things for Carly. The room was full of people visiting Hope and the baby, people who gathered around Carly to ask about her ankle, people who were interested in meeting the new town doctor and his daughter, people—Hope's in-laws—who wanted to show off the most recent addition to Hope's family.

The good thing about the whole situation, Carly thought, was that it gave her a break from Bax and diffused his effect on her. And at that point she was glad for any small favors.

They spent until nearly eight o'clock visiting with everyone before Bax finally cleared the room to examine Hope and the baby. When he had, he, Evie Lee and Carly headed for home again, leaving Hope with her company.

By then Carly had had a long while to lecture herself about how silly she was being over Bax McDermot, and she was convinced she could stop her vulnerability to him if she just put her mind to it.

But putting her mind to it was a whole lot easier when he was at a distance and they were both surrounded by other people than it was when she was sitting at the table in the kitchen of her family home, watching him make mile-high sandwiches for their dinner.

"Nice people," he was saying about the townsfolk he'd just encountered. "I'll bet this whole place is filled with more like them."

"It is," she confirmed, trying not to stare at the

best rear end she'd ever seen as he stood at the counter.

"Your sister and the baby are doing well. I told her she could go home tomorrow."

Carly laughed. "She'd probably rather not. There are three more boys waiting for her there, so her rest will be over."

"True enough," Bax agreed, laughing with her in a deep, rich chuckle that sluiced over the surface of her skin like warm honey.

He brought three plates to the table, complete with sandwiches, chips, pickles and olives, then hollered for Evie Lee to join them as he poured milk for his daughter and iced tea for himself and Carly.

Evie Lee must have been on her way to the kitchen even before the bellow because she popped through the swinging door right then.

"Know what?" she asked her father, her tone full of excitement. "There's a bedroom way up high with pictures all over the walls of castles and mountains and all kinds of stuff. Could it be my room instead of that other one?"

Bax looked to Carly, questioning her with his expression.

"It was my room up until a year or so ago," she explained. "It's in the attic. There's travel posters on the walls."

"Ah," Bax said, nodding. "Is it off-limits?"

"No. Evie Lee can use it if she wants. And if you don't mind having her that far away from you."

"It's not far away," Evie Lee countered. "If I

leave the door open, you could still hear me if I called you.''

''If it's all right with Carly, it's all right with me.''

''Oh goody! Can I eat my dinner up there now? It'll be like a picnic.''

''Okay, but you'll have to be careful with your milk. Come on, you carry your plate and I'll take the glass,'' he instructed before excusing himself from Carly for a moment.

She spent the time he was gone working on her self-control yet again, looking around the warm, familiar country kitchen awash in blue and white, trying to get her bearings. To ground herself.

But then Bax came back and sat across from her at the round mahogany table.

And that was all it took for her to notice the color of his eyes as if for the first time, turning her to mush once more.

''That room is nearly wallpapered in posters,'' he said, referring to her old bedroom as he settled in to eat. ''Are any of those places where you're headed?''

Carly swallowed a bite of sandwich she'd taken to camouflage her latest response to him. ''All of them, with any luck.''

''Looks like you've been planning it for a long time.''

''It seems like forever. Since I wasn't much older than Evie Lee.''

''And just when you were about to leave, this happens.'' He nodded in the direction of her ankle.

"It's only a minor setback."

They both ate some sandwich before Carly picked up the conversational ball and got it rolling again. "Have you traveled at all?"

His eyebrows arched and he nodded as he finished his bite. Then he said, "Some. My brothers and I did a summer-long trip through Europe after I graduated college. I saw most of what you have posters of upstairs and then some. Then I came back here, went to medical school and did a stint in the Peace Corps afterward. Saw Africa that way."

"Wow. And now you want to be in Elk Creek?"

He laughed again. "Don't sound so shocked. I've seen enough to know a small town like this one is still the best place to put down roots, to raise a family. But it's good to go out into the world and have a look at it all before you make that decision if you've a mind to. Helps you to know what's right for you and what's not."

Okay, it was ridiculous, but there was a part of Carly that wasn't happy that he was so in favor of her leaving. She couldn't help feeling as if he were trying to get rid of her.

Or maybe she just would have preferred him trying to convince her to stay.

One way or the other, this whole day since she'd met him had been the strangest of her life.

And she was more than ready to put an end to it.

She'd finished her sandwich, so she pushed the plate away. "I should get going," she announced, even though it seemed as if they'd just started to actually talk to each other and she was cutting that short.

But Bax merely nodded, putting no effort into stopping her from leaving the house, either.

"Are you sure you'll be all right out in the cottage?" he asked.

"I'll be fine," she answered. "Better that than those stairs."

"So, we'll just leave the back door open and you can come and go as you need to use the kitchen— is that how we're doing this?"

"That'll work fine. I shouldn't need anything else—especially upstairs—so you won't have to worry about my being in the hallway when you come out of the shower the way I was today."

He grinned at her, dimpling up again. "That wasn't any big deal. With a daughter in the house I have to be careful about how I walk around anyway."

"Still..." she said, remembering all too vividly the sight of his naked chest and feeling all over again what she'd felt then.

Carly pushed herself to her good foot and put a crutch under each arm.

"So, tomorrow you'll show me my office?" he asked, confirming what they'd mentioned at the medical building when he'd declined the tour of the place.

"Sure."

Bax stood then, too, and went ahead of her to the back door to open it for her. "I sleep with the window open, so if you need me during the night, just call,'' he said as she started to pass through the door.

Needs she was certain were nothing like what he was referring to sprang to the forefront of her mind once more. But all Carly said was, ''I think I'll be fine.''

And then she did something catastrophic.

She glanced up at him as she passed in front of him to get through the door. Close in front of him. And an intense image of him kissing her good-night flooded through her.

This really had been the most bizarre day she'd ever spent.

''See you tomorrow,'' she said in a hurry, forcing herself to look down at the ground instead of up at him and moving the rest of the way out of the house.

But as she hobbled across the breezeway, feeling his eyes following her, she couldn't stop herself from wondering what kind of a kisser he would have been if he actually had kissed her good-night.

And then she could have kicked herself for the thought.

Because something told her that he would be as good at that as he was at handling sprained ankles.

And she had to fight hard against the desire to find out for real.

Chapter Four

As Bax searched the cupboards for a can of coffee the next morning he kept an eye on the guest cottage out back.

The curtains were all pulled and there didn't seem to be any signs that Carly was up and about.

But then it was barely six and there wasn't any reason she should be up that early.

There wasn't any reason *he* should be up that early. Except that he'd dreamed about her and the dream had snapped him awake and left him with such an adrenaline rush he hadn't been able to go back to sleep.

Much as he'd wanted to. To revisit the dream.

Because what a dream it had been!

Carly, stepping out of the bathroom the way he

had the day before. A towel wrapping her naked body. Steam all around. Her hair twisted and held in place with that pencil, just as it had been when he'd first seen her. One long slender arm reaching up to pull the pencil out. Her hair cascading to her still-damp shoulders. A secret smile on that rosebud mouth. Shining topaz eyes giving him a come-hither wink. And then the towel falling away...

Somewhere in recalling the dream Bax had stopped looking for coffee. Instead, he was holding on to the edge of one of the counters like a runner catching his breath.

And he actually did need to catch his breath. Along with calming down the rest of him before anybody walked into the kitchen and saw him in the state the memory had left him.

He straightened, arched his back, and told himself he was being a damn fool.

Then he let out a deep sigh and restarted the search for coffee.

Maybe a hot, dark cup of the stuff would help get him on track again.

Not that anything else had.

"Bingo!" he muttered to himself when he spotted a can of coffee grounds in the same cupboard where the cups were stored.

He took the can down, fiddled with the coffee-maker until he figured it out and then measured the grounds, adding one more scoop than he ordinarily would have in the hope that an extra-strong brew would have some effect on these unwelcome thoughts he'd been having about Carly Winters.

Caffeine as the cure-all.

Once the coffee was on its way he replaced the can and settled in to wait for the liquid to brew.

And as he did, his gaze wandered out the window over the sink to the cottage again.

Was she sleeping? Probably. In pajamas? Or maybe a frilly little nightgown? Or nothing at all...?

"Hurry up, coffee," he said to the machine, desperate for something—anything—to stop the thoughts of Carly.

It had been like this since he'd first set eyes on her the day before. He didn't understand it. And he couldn't curb it. No matter how hard he tried. And he had been trying. But it was as if she were stuck like glue to his brain and he couldn't pry her loose.

Not that it was torturous having her on his mind. Or at least it wouldn't have been if things were different. If he was in the market for a relationship. After all, there was something really appealing about her. She was beautiful and cute at the same time. Thoughtful and independent. Sweet and sexy...

And flustered. She'd been very flustered for some reason.

Maybe she'd sensed the things he'd been thinking about her. The attraction he felt for her.

He'd done his damnedest to hide it. To seem as if he were hardly noticing her at all. But maybe he hadn't done that any better than he'd actually fought his attraction to her. And maybe if she'd sensed it, she'd figured him for some kind of maniac.

Hell, he felt like some kind of maniac.

What rational man would be so bowled over by

a little wisp of a woman he'd just met? What rational man wouldn't be able to stop thinking about her? Wondering how her hair would feel slipping through his fingers. Wondering if he could make her writhe with pleasure if he touched her in just the right spots. Wondering what it would be like to kiss her...

There he was, doing it again. Daydreaming. Night-dreaming. Fantasizing...

What the hell had gotten into him?

He checked the coffeemaker and found the tar-black liquid waiting for him. He filled a mug with steaming coffee, sipping it gingerly rather than allowing it to cool at all.

But that didn't help, either.

Carly was still right there in his mind's eye. Skin like fresh cream. The thickest eyelashes he'd ever seen. Those perky little breasts...

"Geez," he groaned at himself and his own inability to escape his mental wanderings.

It was as if he'd suddenly developed some kind of obsession with her. Like a starving man craving a steak and not being able to think about anything else until he got one. No doubt about it, he felt like a starving man. And she was definitely the lean, succulent steak he was craving.

He drank more coffee, flinching at the scalding his esophagus took as punishment.

It was just a damn good thing Carly was leaving town, he decided, or he was liable to be the worst doctor Elk Creek had ever seen. Preoccupied. Distracted. All het up...

That was why he'd encouraged those travel plans of hers that had been postponed because of her ankle. With the way things had been so far, her leaving Elk Creek had started to seem like his only chance for salvation. Too bad he couldn't put her on the first train out of there.

But fast on that thought came a gnawing in his gut that let him know that wasn't really what he wanted at all.

Okay, so maybe a part of him wanted her to stick around. Wanted to get to know her. Wanted to delve deeper into what he'd so far only seen on the surface. Wanted to explore what made her tick. To know if she was as wholesome and homespun as she seemed, as fresh and funny, as bright and beguilingly sexy.

Sexy again...

He seemed to have *that* on the brain, too.

But no matter what he wanted, he reminded himself sternly, the last thing he *needed* was a woman in his life right now. Let alone a woman he couldn't stop thinking about. A woman he couldn't even escape in his sleep. A woman he was itching to see when he wasn't with her. Itching to touch when he was.

A woman with an agenda of her own that didn't mesh with his.

"Been there, done that."

And he wasn't going to do it again.

No, what he *was* going to do was keep on fighting the attraction he had for Carly because there was just no place for it. Not in his life and not in hers.

And while he was waging the battle, he'd hold on to the hope that the attraction wasn't bigger than he was.

Although at that moment, standing there staring across the breezeway at the cottage once more and imagining himself slipping in to watch her sleep, waking her with a soft kiss, he wasn't convinced that what was happening with him wasn't already a little out of hand.

Plain blue jeans. A simple white, short-sleeve, V-neck T-shirt. Her hair in a French braid. Just a little light mascara, blush and lip gloss.

Carly was absolutely certain she had herself under control as she made her way across the breezeway to let Bax know she was ready to go with him to the medical building and show him his office.

No more fluttering insides. No more weak knees. No more goose bumps. No more of anything that had plagued her the day and evening before. She was her old self. She'd avoided the temptation to wear something special and made sure to dress the way she would have for any other sunny Monday morning. And she was convinced that the whole attraction thing was just some kind of fluke she had finally overcome with a good night's sleep.

Then Bax opened the main house's back door in answer to her knock.

And there he was, dressed not much differently than she was in snug-fitting denim jeans that hugged his hips and stretched taut with the hard bulge of well-developed thighs, a work-worn chambray shirt with the sleeves rolled to his biceps and a pair of cowboy boots more suited to ranching than to doctoring. He smelled of that clean, spicy soap again, and as she breathed it in he smiled at her with those dimples and those great green eyes. And the whole package hit her like a ton of bricks.

So much for being in control and back to her old self.

She even swayed on her crutches as she stood there, to such an extent that he reached for her with both hands on her shoulders to steady her. Hands that seemed to sear right through her shirt and brand her.

Lord, but she wished this reaction to him would stop!

"Ready to go?" she asked cheerily, drawing herself up stiffly enough to slip from his grip.

"Sure. Are you okay this morning?"

Even a slight frown beetling his brow only added to the man's handsomeness. Damn him anyway.

"I'm fine," she answered too brightly, overcompensating.

"You look good," he said, his gaze going from head to toe to head again, broadening his smile and leaving her wondering if he was flirting.

But before she had a chance to decide, he glanced over his shoulder and yelled, "Evie Lee! Let's go. Carly's here." And his young daughter came barreling through the kitchen's swinging door.

"Carly's here?" she repeated as if Carly were a gift-laden Santa Claus come to pay her a midyear visit.

"Good morning, sweetie," Carly said, appreciating the delighted welcome and the diversion from Bax.

"Oh, let me see your hair today!" the little girl demanded effusively, charging around her father, out the door and around to Carly's back. "That's so pretty and fancy, too! Can you do that to me?"

"Sure. It's just a braid."

"Daddy can't do things like that."

"How about playing beauty shop later?" Bax said to his daughter. "Carly came to take us to my new office right now."

"Can we do my hair later?" Evie Lee asked Carly.

"As soon as we get back," Carly promised.

"Then let's go so we can hurry up and come home."

The two adults followed the child's lead, heading down the same path they'd taken the night before.

Along the way Bax asked how Carly's ankle was today and she told him it was better, even though, in actuality, it was more swollen and black and blue than it had been. She was afraid if she told him the truth, he might want to examine it. And if he examined it, that meant he might touch it. And she knew too well how powerful his touch could be.

Nice. Gentle. Warm. Arousing.

Definitely much, much too powerful to leave her with a clear head. And she was determined to keep her head clear, if it was the last thing she did.

But in the process of thinking about keeping a clear head, Carly made the mistake of bringing Bax into the medical building through the front door rather than the rear. Unlike the previous night when the only other people in the place had been in Hope's room on the upper floor, today there were folks milling around everywhere.

Tallie Shanahan—who had been handling all minor medical treatments since arriving in town only a few weeks earlier—was just calling a patient to one of the examining rooms when Carly, Bax and Evie Lee entered the building. Tallie would soon be Bax's sister-in-law since she was engaged to his brother Ry, but Carly knew that Tallie had only met Bax over the telephone during his interview. So when Tallie glanced up at the threesome as if they were more patients, Carly had to introduce Bax. Once she did that—with the whole waiting room within hearing range—Tallie had no choice but to do a general introduction to the half-dozen people eavesdropping. And despite the fact that the introduction included the information that he wasn't there to work yet and was taking a few days to get his bearings, people were eager to shake his hand and tell him their ailments.

Carly was a doctor's daughter so she knew this came with the territory. And since it was her fault that she'd brought him in the way she had and made him fair game, she also knew she had to be the one to ease him through the waiting room as best she could.

It was no simple task, but as Tallie went on to see patients, Carly finally managed to get Bax, Evie Lee and herself through the door behind the reception desk and into the hallway that led to the office and the examining rooms.

"The office is at the end of the hall," she said, leading the way.

It had been her father's office for forty-four years, until his death six months ago. Carly had been in it since then, but only when she, her mother and sister had cleared her dad's things out of the old scarred walnut desk not long after the sudden heart attack that took his life.

Crossing the threshold into the office now was more emotionally difficult than she'd expected as memories of her father flooded her.

She put some effort into shaking them off by facing Bax from the center of the room and apologizing for not bringing him in the back way. But the whole time he was assuring her it was all right, she could feel the urge to escape this place that had been the very essence of her dad.

"Let me point out a few things," she said, hating that she sounded so fragile. "And then I'll get out of here so you can do whatever it is you want to do here."

She cleared her throat when what she was actually trying to do was strengthen her voice. Then she continued. "The key to the desk drawers is in the top one. That same key locks and unlocks the credenza. I guess they've always been a set. We cleared my dad's stuff out of them both so they're all yours—"

Her voice cracked at the mention of her father and it seemed to alert Bax to how tough this was for her. He took over.

"I saw the shelves of patient files behind the reception desk, so I'm figurin' that's where they're kept, and Stella—if I'm rememberin' her name right—the receptionist, will likely be the one to ask for any of those I might need. Right?"

Carly nodded.

He pointed his chin in the direction of the old leather sofa that was against the wall facing the desk. "My guess is that that couch has seen its fair share of catnaps. Those bare nails on that wall over there are where your father's diplomas were hung and where mine will go. But I noticed there's no screen on the window. Is that because he climbed out of it once or twice to give himself a breather without having to explain it?"

That made Carly smile, which she was reasonably sure had been the point of the unrealistic assumption. But she was just grateful that his joke helped diffuse some of her tension. "I think the screen is just being fixed, but sneaking out the window is probably not a bad idea."

Bax walked to the wall that faced the desk. The worn leather sofa against it had seen better days, but what drew his attention was the wall itself. Floor to ceiling, end to end, it was a collage of photographs.

"Explain this for me, though, would you?"

Carly hobbled to stand beside him as Evie Lee climbed onto the couch to get a better look, too.

"Wow, look at all those pi'tures."

"It started with the first baby my dad delivered," Carly informed them both. "He took a snapshot of the family and pinned it up here so he could see it whenever he wanted. He was so proud of that very first new Elk Creek citizen he'd helped bring into the world. The pictures just snowballed from there. It got to be a tradition. Not only for him to take photographs of new babies, but of new patients, and kids—or even grown-ups—in fresh casts or when the casts came off broken arms or legs. Of people he helped one way or another. Sometimes, even if folks moved out of town, they'd send him pictures with notes on how they were doing and he'd put those up, too. It got to be sort of a goal for everyone to have their picture on Dad's wall. I suppose you could say this is the gallery of his practice. Of most of his life. We didn't have the heart to take it down.''

Tears suddenly sprang to Carly's eyes. She blinked them back and in spite of the fact that Bax had been studying the photographs and not looking at her, he seemed to sense the wellspring of emotion that had been tapped.

Without so much as glancing at her or taking his eyes off the wall, he reached a hand to her back and rubbed it softly.

The gesture was no more than an offer of comfort and that was how she took it. But it was an offer of comfort that melted something inside her. Something more than the sensual awakening it brought with it, more than the sparks it lit in her at his touch.

It melted some of the internal starch she'd been using to resist him and she wanted badly to turn to him, to lay her cheek against his vast chest and feel him engulf her in those oh-so-able arms.

And that was when she knew she was in real trouble with this man. Because not only was he drop-dead gorgeous and so sexy it seemed to infuse the air around him, he was also a nice person. A compassionate person. A person, like her father, who would be a good doctor for Elk Creek.

"Of course you're free to take the pictures down now that the office is yours," she said softly when she had some control of herself again.

Bax slid his hand up to her neck, gave a slight squeeze and let go.

"I like it," he said, still studying the wall. "It'll be a great icebreaker when I ask patients to pick themselves out for me. Besides, it's a sort of legacy, isn't it? And legacies shouldn't be tampered with."

There wasn't anything more right he could have said and Carly finally hazarded a glance at him. "Thanks," she murmured.

"Nothin' to thank me for," he claimed, meeting her eyes with his.

For a moment Carly lost herself in those green depths. The urge to turn into his embrace only got stronger and in that same moment something seemed to connect them. To isolate them from everything else and leave them in the center of their own universe.

Carly had the oddest sensation that there was something predestined about this whole thing. Predestined and out of her hands...

"Can we go home now?"

Evie Lee was part of what Carly had forgotten about, but the sound of the child's voice reminded her that Bax's daughter was still very much with them. It seemed as if Bax had also lost track of Evie Lee because the little girl's question snapped him out of that moment of silent reverie, too.

Bax looked away first, but not in any hurry and clearly reluctantly.

"I told you we were going to need to spend some time here, Evie," he said to his daughter.

"But I want Carly to do my hair."

Before either Carly or Bax could comment about that, Tallie knocked on the door they'd left open and said, "I'm sorry, Bax. I know you didn't come in to see patients today, but I have a few out here who are insisting they have emergencies that can only be taken care of by a doctor now that they know there's one on the premises."

Bax chuckled good-naturedly. "It's okay. I'll see them."

"Thanks," Tallie said as if he'd answered her prayers, then disappeared as quietly as she'd come.

"That's my fault," Carly acknowledged. "If I'd brought you in the other way, no one would know you were here and you wouldn't have to go to work before you're ready to. So how about this. I'm going upstairs to see Hope and the baby before they leave and Evie Lee could come with me. Then we'll go back to the house and braid her hair and I'll keep her busy while you take care of things here."

"I don't expect you to be my baby-sitter."

"But finding one is probably one of the things you were going to do before you thought you'd have to start dealing with patients, isn't it?"

"Yeah," he admitted. "But still—"

"I don't mind. Besides, Evie Lee can be a big help to me while I'm on these things." Carly raised one crutch to demonstrate what she was referring to.

"I can get stuff for her and help her with stuff, too," Evie Lee chimed in, clearly liking the idea.

Bax lovingly roughed up his daughter's hair. "You promise you'll behave yourself and do everything Carly tells you?"

Evie Lee nodded vigorously.

"And you're sure you don't mind?" he asked Carly.

"I'm positive."

"Okay, then. I appreciate it."

"Oh goody, goody, goody," Evie Lee cheered, leaping off the sofa. "Let's go."

"I guess I'll see you ladies at home in a little while," Bax said.

"There's no rush," Carly assured him as she made her way to the door.

But before she left the office something caused her to turn and look back at Bax where he stood in the center of the room.

Even though she still had pangs of loss, she felt as if she'd handed over what her father had loved dearly to someone her dad would have approved of. And liked.

Almost as much as she did.

Chapter Five

Word traveled like wildfire in Elk Creek, so it was no surprise to Carly that by midafternoon there were patients lined up around the block to see Bax. The town had been a long time without a doctor and even though Tallie had done a good job since moving back, even though there had been an occasional week of a visiting doctor's care, there was a fair share of the population who felt their medical needs had gone unattended.

Carly was racked with guilt for having been the cause of the avalanche of patients to befall Bax, so when he called at five to say he still had a waiting room jam-packed with people and didn't know when he'd get home, she assured him there was no hurry, that she was enjoying Evie Lee's company, and that they would have dinner waiting for him when he got there.

But when he got there, *they* weren't waiting for him. Only Carly was because it was nearly ten o'clock and Evie Lee had fallen asleep on the couch in the living room.

Carly was sitting at the other end of the sofa watching the child sleep when she heard the back door open. She told herself that the speed with which she got to her good foot, onto her crutches and headed for the kitchen was merely because she didn't want Bax to come into the living room and wake his daughter.

But deep down she was fighting a rise of pure eagerness to see him again.

Bax was standing at the sink when she slipped through the swinging door. He was facing away from her, washing his hands. With the water running, he didn't hear her come in.

She should have announced herself, but for a moment she just stood there, her already intense attraction to him strengthening with every second.

It wasn't the width of his shoulders in the chambray shirt. It wasn't the narrowing of his waist. It wasn't even that derriere that was so remarkable. It was something about the back of his legs. Long, thick, hard legs, spread slightly apart, sexy and so strong they looked as if they could brace the weight of the world.

And Carly had an image of them bare of the tight jeans, straddling her...

"Hi," she said softly, yanking her gaze upward

and hoping that if she let him know she was there it would help push away the image, the thoughts, the desire.

Bax glanced over his shoulder at her as he turned off the water and reached for a paper towel from the holder underneath the cupboard to dry his hands.

"Hi," he answered as he turned and leaned against the counter's edge.

His chiseled jaw was whiskered with the full day's growth of beard, and it only added to his appeal in her eyes. He looked rough and rugged and more masculine than she could bear.

She knew she should tell him what he needed to know, say good-night and get out of there, but she'd been so hungry to see him again since they'd parted that morning that she just couldn't make herself do it. And despite telling herself she owed him a little company while he ate, it was nothing more than a feeble excuse when the truth was that she just couldn't resist having her own hunger satisfied.

"I made a casserole. It's still in the oven," she said, trying not to feast on him with her eyes. But that wasn't easy. Five-o'clock shadow or no five-o'clock shadow, he didn't look any the worse for wear. There were hardly any signs that he'd just put in a twelve-hour day. Instead, his green eyes were as bright as ever and if anything, he seemed even more at ease.

"Great. I'm starved," he said in answer to her announcement.

But Carly was so lost in the sight of him that it

took her a moment to recall what he was responding to.

When she did, she crossed to the stove, propped both crutches under one arm and used a hot pad to take the dish out of the oven.

Setting it on the stove top was as far as she got before Bax came to lend a hand. "Let me do this. And while I eat, let's soak that ankle of yours. I brought a footbath and some Epsom salts from the office."

Oh good, a valid reason for staying.

"Go sit at the table and let me set it up," he instructed.

She did as she was told, unwrapping the bandage while Bax filled the footbath and brought it to her.

He made sure the water level was high enough and the temperature just right, then he returned to the stove for the casserole.

"There's salad in the fridge and beer or iced tea to drink," she informed him as he put the dish on the table near the plate, napkin and silverware she'd arranged for him when she and Evie Lee had eaten.

He made a second trip for the salad, a jar of Caesar dressing she'd made and the tea.

"Can I get you something?" he asked.

"No, thanks. I'm fine."

Carly watched him serve himself, and while she did she said, "Evie Lee is sleeping on the couch. She tried to wait up for you, but she didn't make it."

"I figured she was down for the count. She never

stays awake past nine, no matter how determined she is. But I hate it when I miss her.''

"That's my fault. I really am sorry about today. I know better than to bring the doctor in the front door,'' she apologized for her faux pas again.

"It's okay. There were a few folks who really did need to be seen. And much as I wish it wasn't true, Evie is pretty used to my working late. Besides, I'm not worried that this will be the norm, so don't beat yourself up over it.''

Carly appreciated how he was taking the whole thing.

She also appreciated the sight of him eating, that sleek jaw working as he chewed....

"Good stuff,'' he complimented when his mouth wasn't full.

The hamburger, green beans and gravy casserole with mashed potatoes on top was hardly gourmet fare. "You're probably just starved,'' she said with a laugh.

"That, too,'' he agreed, dimpling up for her. "How did you spend the day?'' he asked then.

"Hope and the baby were on their way out when we got upstairs, so we went along home with them. Evie Lee got to meet my nephews—they're two, three and four—and being the advanced age of six herself, she mothered them all.''

"Ordered them around is more like it.''

"That, too,'' Carly agreed with him, laughing again. "We had lunch over there and then came home when it was everybody's nap time. Evie Lee swore she doesn't take naps anymore, so I didn't make her—I hope that was okay.''

"She was right, she doesn't take them. She barely took them when she was a baby. So what did you do when you got here?"

"We did her hair and I read to her and we colored and that took up the afternoon. Then we fixed supper and put a puzzle together and she fell asleep in the middle of my reading to her again tonight.''

"Sounds like a full day.''

"Not as full as yours, but full enough.''

"I hope she didn't wear you out or keep you on that foot too much.''

"No on both counts. She didn't wear me out, I had a great time with her, and she didn't keep me on my feet too much because she waited on me every chance she got. Of course, I had to call her Nurse Evie Lee Lewis, but that was just part of the game.''

It was Bax's turn to laugh. "Sounds like she played nurse while you played teacher.''

"I wasn't playing. I am a teacher.''

"Ah, that explains it. Of little kids?''

"Junior high. Geography.''

He nodded knowingly. "I should have guessed that one. Goes along with that wanderlust of yours.''

"Mmm,'' she agreed, wishing *wander*lust was the only kind she was feeling these days.

Bax had finished eating by then and cleared the table, leaving the dishes in the sink so he could rejoin her. He sat in the same chair he'd used before, but this time he lounged in it, draping one arm over the back of it and stretching the other out on the tabletop.

Carly suddenly found herself interested in the coarse hair that speckled thick forearms and wrists, another element of his masculinity that thrummed something sensual inside her.

"Would you mind telling me about your dad?" he asked then. "It's looking like I have some pretty big shoes to fill."

That made Carly smile and helped her rein in her thoughts.

She forced her glance up to his face once more. "You do have big shoes to fill," she told him kindly, but in no uncertain terms.

"Your father's patients surely do miss him."

"He was a good man. An old-fashioned country doctor who knew his patients inside and out. He loved them and they loved him."

"I got that message today. Even my genuinely ill patients spent as much time tellin' me how great he was as they did tellin' me how sick they were. Was your dad a hometown boy?"

"Born and raised. So's my mom. They always said that being an Elk Creek native made it hard for Dad to be taken seriously when he first started his practice here. Some folks wouldn't even go to him right off the bat. They said they knew him when he was an ornery, mischief-making kid, so how could they turn around and trust him with their health care? He almost didn't stay because of it. He and Mom were thinking about leaving Elk Creek—or so the story goes."

"What changed their minds?"

"Mom got pregnant with Hope, for one. They didn't want to raise a family anywhere else. And a few emergencies came up that proved Dad's salt. Little by little, folks came around. Like they will with you, if you're worrying about it because they gave you a rough time today."

Bax's grin let her know she'd hit the nail on the head. "And your dad ended up being loved by all," Bax finished for her.

"He was always loved by all. It just took some time to be loved and trusted as a doctor."

"But when it kicked in, it kicked in but good, from what I heard today."

Carly conceded that. "My dad had two things going for him—he really, truly cared about these people, and he was the kind of man who made sure nobody in town went without a turkey for Thanksgiving or toys for their kids on Christmas. He saw being a doctor as more than just pill pushing. He *talked* to his patients. He made them all friends. He found out what was going on in their lives, in their heads, in their hearts, so he had the whole picture. He was like a father to everybody, I guess."

"And how was he as a father to you?"

"Oh, he was good at that, too. I can't remember more than a handful of nights in my whole growing-up years when he wasn't home to tuck me in. Even if it just meant running over for five minutes from sitting at someone's bedside, he'd make sure he was home to tell me to have sweet dreams."

"Are you sure he didn't climb out that office window to do it?'' Bax asked with a laugh, clearly thinking of the day he'd just put in and the impossibility of getting away himself.

"Maybe he did and that's why the screen is in such bad shape,'' she agreed, playing along. "I'm just saying that my dad was really conscious not to forget about his family. If he'd been away a lot or one of us kids felt as if we hadn't seen enough of him, he'd let us spend a day at the office with him, being his assistant—even if we had to ditch school to do it.''

"Sounds like he was quite a guy.''

"He was.''

"Kind of like his daughter is quite a woman.''

That came out of the blue and brought a blush to Carly's cheeks. "I don't know about that,'' she said, deflecting the compliment and wishing she could as easily deflect the steady stare of his eyes as she realized that he hadn't taken them off her the whole while they'd been talking.

As the heat from his gaze seeped all through her, it made her aware of just how cold the water in the footbath had become and that gave her another diversion.

"I think my ankle has soaked long enough. The water's getting pretty cool.''

Even that didn't cause an instant reaction. For a moment Bax just went on studying her, smiling a small, secret smile, as if he liked what he saw.

But then he bent over and dipped a finger in the water to test it.

"Yep, cold, all right. Better get you out of there.''

"There are towels on the shelf above the dryer in the laundry room," she informed him.

The laundry room was just off the kitchen to the right and Bax was back with towel in hand before she'd done more than raise her foot out of the now chilly bath.

He hunkered down in front of her the way he had the night before and scooped her foot into the towel, a medical version of Prince Charming trying on Cinderella's glass slipper.

"I can do that," Carly said as he began to blot her skin dry, careful not to press too hard and hurt her.

But Bax went right on doing it, studying the increased swelling and bruising while he was at it.

"I know it looks worse," she said, trying to keep her own perspective and not lose herself too much in the pleasure of his ministrations. No matter how tempting it was to just sit back and indulge in the tenderness of his touch.

"Par for the course," he answered. "It may look even worse tomorrow, but then it should start to improve. You did one hell of a job on it."

"You can leave it unwrapped. I have a clean bandage at the cottage and I can wrap it myself over there," she said then, almost afraid of what any more contact with him would inspire in her.

"Okay," he agreed, slipping the bath out of the way so she could gingerly set her foot on the towel he laid out on the floor.

As he took the bath to empty in the laundry tub,

Carly gathered up the used bandage, put it in her pocket and got up onto her crutches again.

"You don't have to go," Bax said, returning from the laundry room for the second time. "It can stay unwrapped for a little while." He seemed disappointed at the obvious sign that she was ending the evening.

"It feels better if it's wrapped. Besides, you've had a long day. I'm sure you want to relax."

He grinned at her with a hint of the devil in the corners of his supple mouth. "Who said I wasn't relaxed?"

"You know what I mean."

Carly headed for the back door and Bax crossed with her on just a few strides of those long legs she'd had unholy visions of earlier.

As they reached the door and went out into the breezeway, he said, "I understand there are some folks I should see on a couple of the outlying spreads around here. I called the ranch to let my family know I was in town but wouldn't be able to get there today the way I'd planned, but we arranged for me to take Evie out there to stay tomorrow while I do some travelin' to the other places. Gives me a chance to get an idea of what all I'm lookin' at and see whatever folks I need to. Then I'll go on back to the ranch for dinner."

Carly didn't know why he was outlining his next day's plans for her, but she did know the thought of him being busy and away and her not getting to see him deflated her spirits much more than it should have.

"Sounds good," she said without any enthusiasm.

"I also heard from more than one source today that you're pretty popular with folks around here, particularly with some of the older ones. I was told that you used to do house calls with your dad when you could and that havin' you along would be a feather in my cap when I go to introduce myself to some of the less sociable souls out in the country-side. Not to mention that I could use a guide to give directions to find these people. Think I could persuade you to come along?" he concluded, finally getting to the point.

The air was pumped back into Carly just that quick. Even though she knew it shouldn't have been.

He'd made the request sound innocent enough. Harmless enough. But Carly knew better. She knew that any time spent with him was dangerous because she liked him too much. Because for some reason she didn't understand, she was particularly suscep-tible to him.

So, just say no, she told herself.

But saying no meant just what she'd thought be-fore—it meant he would go off tomorrow and do his business and she wouldn't see him at all.

And she hated that eventuality so much, she couldn't inflict it on herself even if it *was* what she *should* do.

"What do you say?" he persisted, making her realize she'd let too much of a pause linger while she argued with herself.

"Sure. I don't have anything else to do tomorrow,'' she heard herself say before she was completely sure she was going to agree.

''Great. I'd really appreciate it. We don't have to go too early, though. Maybe around eleven?''

''Fine.''

Great. Fine. No problem. Except for the racing of her heart at just the idea of the next day and being with him again.

Carly crossed the breezeway, wishing it were about a mile longer so maybe the night air could have more chance of cooling her off.

Although if Bax went along—the way he was going along now—no amount of distance would have helped.

When they reached the cottage, he opened the door for her, but he stood half blocking it so she couldn't go in. Instead, she was left facing him, looking up into eyes that seemed to delve into her.

''Thanks for taking care of Evie Lee today and tonight. And for the supper.''

''No thanks necessary. I enjoyed it.'' And him. Everything about him...

He went right on staring down at her, studying her face as if he were learning it.

Then, when she least expected it, he raised a hand to brush the backs of his fingers against her cheek in a feathery stroke.

''I hope I didn't upset you by asking you to talk about your dad.''

She shook her head. Upset was definitely *not* how she was feeling. ''Being in his office was a little hard, but talking about him only brings back good memories.''

Bax nodded. Slowly. Never taking his eyes off her.

''I really do appreciate everything you did today,'' he repeated, this time in a voice that had gone deeper, softer, more intimate.

''No big deal,'' she responded, her own voice joining the intimacy.

He went on looking at her in a way that seemed to draw her to him. That seemed to block out everything else, leaving them alone in that space and time.

And then he leaned in closer and kissed her.

It was just a brief peck of a kiss, although it wasn't timid or abrupt or the way a young boy might snatch a smooch from a young girl.

It was confident. Smooth. Intriguing.

It was just short.

But not so short that it wasn't enough to give her a taste of lips that felt even better than they looked. Enough to set a whole lot of things in her atwitter.

Then he smiled down at her again, looking pleased with himself. Or maybe with her. Or with the kiss. Or maybe with everything all rolled together.

''Night, Carly,'' he said.

''Good night,'' she answered, hating that her voice sounded so small, so starstruck.

He stepped out of her way then and said, ''See you in the morning,'' and left her on the threshold of the cottage.

But somehow she felt as if she were on the threshold of more than just the guest house.

And as she stepped inside she couldn't help wondering what a full-fledged kiss from him would do to her if just a peck could leave her feeling as if a whole new door had just opened in her life.

Chapter Six

Carly had never been a late sleeper so when Deana knocked on the cottage door at ten the next morning and called, "It's me," Carly was already up, showered and dressed in a sunny yellow, cap-sleeve A-line dress that went all the way to her ankles. She was in the process of fastening her hair only inches from the ends with an elastic ruffle to hang in a low, loose ponytail, so she merely yelled back, "The door's open."

"I come bearing fresh bagels and cream cheese," Deana said as she let herself in.

One look at Carly standing in front of the mirror on the bathroom door and Deana added, "Wow! How come you're all dressed up?"

"I'm not 'all dressed up.' This is just a sundress."

"That you usually reserve for summer parties."

"I have to go with Bax to introduce him to the people on the farms and ranches outside of town and then have dinner at his family's place. I don't want to do all that in jeans."

Deana's well-shaped eyebrows reached for her hairline. "One day I don't see you and you're calling him Bax as if the two of you are old friends and he's taking you to eat with his whole family?"

"It isn't the way you're making it sound," Carly said as she sat at the table and pointed to the other chair for Deana.

Carly had pushed her open suitcase to the wall so half the table was usable, and she'd set her carry-on bag on the floor to free both chairs, mainly thinking of Evie Lee but now accommodating Deana, too.

Deana set the sack she was carrying on the table, produced two cups of coffee from it, two cranberry bagels and a small tub of cream cheese. Then she sat down herself.

"How's your ankle? I wanted to get over here yesterday, but my sister had a crisis—Clive broke up with her. I had to rush over there at the crack of dawn and didn't get home until after midnight last night."

"That's okay. There isn't anything you can do here anyway. It's just a matter of time and hobbling around on the crutches."

"Does it hurt much?"

"Sometimes, if I try to put any weight on it or when the bandage is off, but it's not a big deal. How's your sister? I know she was thinking she and

Clive were on the verge of getting engaged. She must be heartbroken.''

''She is. But we both know she's better off without him and I think she'll see that when the worst of the shock is over.'' Deana took a sip of coffee and changed the subject. ''Now, what's going on with you and the good doctor?'' she demanded with the same inflection she'd use if Carly was about to tell her the principal of the school where they both worked was moonlighting as a drug smuggler.

''There's nothing *going on* with me and the good doctor. I just seem to have inherited the job of showing him around and introducing him to everyone.''

''Which means spending a lot of time with him,'' Deana concluded as they divvied up the cream cheese and started to eat.

''It's kind of hard not to spend time with him under the circumstances. He's living in my house and we're sharing the kitchen. He's taken over my dad's practice. And he's also looking after my ankle.''

''You lucky dog you.''

Deana's envious sigh made Carly recall that her friend had seemed to have quite an appreciation for Bax when they'd all initially met on the front lawn the other morning.

It also restirred the twinge of jealousy Carly had felt, but she didn't want to think about that.

''Did you kind of have your eye on Bax?'' Carly asked tentatively, unsure exactly what to say, but thinking she should somehow address the subject.

Deana waved a hand at her as if she were shooing

away a fly. "I thought he was drop-dead gorgeous and the best hunk to hit town in a while. But if he's managed to snare your interest, that's even better. You can have him and maybe he'll have a friend for me. It could all work out great!"

"He hasn't managed to snare my interest," Carly protested too much. "But if he had, why would that be even better and make things work out great?"

"Because if you fall head over heels for our new town doctor, you'll stay in Elk Creek. And I'm all in favor of anything that makes that happen, even if it means you get the guy and I don't."

"Deana—"

"I know. You're going to say you let a man tie you to this town once and you won't do it again. But I can hope, can't I? Besides, Bax McDermot is a whole lot more man than Jeremy ever was. He'd be worth being pinned to Elk Creek for eternity."

There was no disputing that Bax was more man than Carly's former fiancé had been. There wasn't any comparison at all.

But she didn't want to think about Bax's good qualities any more than she wanted to think about that dumb jealousy twinge.

As she and Deana sat eating their bagels, though, Carly knew it would have been the perfect time to encourage her friend to go after Bax. Maybe even to offer to set them up on a blind date.

Yet Carly just couldn't make herself do that.

No matter how hard she tried.

"You do like him, though, don't you?" Deana said then as if she were reading Carly's mind.

"There's nothing *not* to like. He's nice, under-
standing, kind, compassionate, caring, considerate.
He has a good sense of humor, great hands. He's a
good father—"

"Hold it. What was that *great hands* part?"

That had slipped out. Carly had been hoping Deana wouldn't catch it.

"Surgeon's hands. It just meant that he'll be able
to do operations well when he needs to."

Deana laughed out loud. "That is *not* what you
meant. Has he gotten his hands on you already?"

"On my ankle. Only in a medical capacity."

"And you liked it, didn't you? And not in just a
medical capacity."

"So he's gentle. So what?"

Deana smiled like a kid who'd just found pre-
cisely what she asked for under the Christmas tree.
"This is better than I thought."

Carly rolled her eyes. "Deana, as soon as my ankle heals, I'm leaving Elk Creek just the way I
planned. And no man—not even Bax McDermot—
is going to change that. I let that happen before, and
I will not let it happen again," she said forcefully.

"We'll see."

"I mean it."

"Okay. You mean it," Deana conceded without
conceding anything at all because she was still smiling like the cat that ate the canary.

*So prove you mean what you say and fix her up
with Bax,* a little voice in the back of Carly's mind
challenged her.

But in that instant when Carly imagined the new

doctor's hands on her friend—in any way, medical or not—in that instant when Carly imagined Bax giving Deana even the kind of almost-nothing kiss he'd given her the night before, Carly's hackles rose so high she still couldn't make herself do it.

And worse than that, she almost felt a hint of an inclination to actually stay in Elk Creek to keep it from happening.

"This is crazy," she said, not realizing the words were going to come out until they had.

But Deana took them as a comment on their conversation, unaware that Carly was talking to herself about her own thoughts.

"Crazy or not, I'll take what I can get when it comes to any chance of you not leaving," Deana said. "And crazier things than this have happened. With Bax McDermot in town, Elk Creek may have a whole new appeal for you."

"Please don't get your hopes up, Deana," Carly beseeched.

But she could see that her friend's hopes were already up.

And as much as Carly didn't want to admit it, she knew something was up with her, too.

She just didn't know quite what it was.

"So what, besides the lollipops you haven't offered me yet, is in the bag?" Bax asked with a nod at the paper grocery sack near Carly's feet as she sat in the passenger seat of his car.

They'd stopped at the McDermot ranch to say a brief hello to his family, then left Evie Lee to the afternoon her uncles had planned for her, an afternoon of playing with the animals and riding the horses.

Carly had dipped into the bag to send a rainbow-colored sucker with the little girl for later, and now that Carly and Bax were on their way to the outlying farms and ranches, Bax's curiosity about the grocery sack she had packed before they left seemed to have gotten the better of him.

Carly glanced at him, trying not to notice how good he looked in his khaki-colored jeans and crisp white shirt with the sleeves rolled to his elbows.

"I'm sorry. I didn't think you'd want a sucker."

"Think again," he advised with an ornery smile tossed her way as he drove down the deserted country road.

Carly reached into the sack and produced the same kind of lollipop she'd given his daughter. She unwrapped it and held it out to him.

Rather than taking it with his hand, he leaned over and took it with his mouth, grinning up at her before straightening in the seat and focusing once again on the road.

It was a playfully intimate gesture that warmed Carly more than she wanted to admit. Especially since they were alone in the middle of nowhere, in the close confines of his station wagon.

She forced her own eyes straight ahead, too, trying not to be so aware of the way he moved the candy around in his mouth.

When he'd settled it in the bulge of one cheek, he said, "So, what are we in for this afternoon?"

Talking about that seemed like safe territory. And Carly was grateful for anything that might keep her mind off the heady scent of his aftershave filling the sun-warmed interior of the car and infusing her with too strong a sense of his masculinity.

She jumped right into the subject.

"Be prepared for plenty of stories about sprains, broken bones and months on crutches. Having me along will inspire everyone who's ever had a similar injury to tell you about it."

"Great. It'll give us a good opening. Who's up first?"

"The Marris family. Their farm is about four more miles out. They have eleven kids and another on the way—that's who the lollipops are mainly for. Three of the kids are prone to strep throat and four to ear infections, and even though they're great, well-behaved kids, it helps to have a reward waiting after you examine them."

"I'll remember that. Twelve kids, huh?"

"They wanted a big family."

"I'd say a dozen kids qualifies. What's the age range?"

"Eighteen months to seventeen, with two sets of twins in the mix. But you'll always find the kids and the house spotlessly clean, and they come into town every Sunday for church."

"So they're good people is what you're telling me."

"Good enough that we all try to make things easier for them if we can. Sometimes Kansas—she owns the general store—opens up just for them after the Sunday service if they haven't been able to get in to do their shopping any other time. And my dad met them at the office after church, too, on occasion, if one of them was under the weather. They're nice enough folks to do a little extra to help them out. And if you do, it'll be worth your while. Helen Marris makes the best zucchini bread in the county and she'll reward you with a loaf for your trouble.''

"Okay. I like zucchini bread as much as the next guy."

"Good. I'm glad to know you'll do what you can to help out, too. I think that's what being a small-town doctor is all about—being flexible, taking an extra step now and then."

Bax pretended to strain for a glimpse into the sack. "So, that accounts for the suckers. But I can tell there's more than that in there."

"There's a couple of fishing magazines for Murray Abrams—the old issues nobody's reading in the waiting room anymore. Some people call him Murray the Grouch because he's so cantankerous. Don't be surprised if he greets us with a shotgun and even shoots a load over our heads before he realizes who we are. But don't let it phase you. It's a test of your mettle. He really isn't such an ogre when you get to know him."

"He's the diabetic Tallie told me about."

"Right. But the other thing is that you can't *ever* let him see a needle. Dad was able to treat his diabetes with oral meds so far and it's a good thing because I don't know what would happen if he had to use injections. If you have to give him a shot for any reason, make sure he's lying flat on his back on the bed because he passes out cold.''

"Okay. Good to know.''

Carly continued with her roll call of the patients Bax would be meeting today. ''There are quite a few elderly people. It's not unusual for these big spreads to be passed down to the kids and grandkids—''

"The way ours was.''

"Right. And a lot of the older folks have stayed on to live. There's one couple—the Krupcheks— who are both in their nineties and in a constant state of World War III. They'll tell you they're getting a divorce and one or the other of them will try to talk us into taking them into town to live with some of their other relatives. But if you cajole them a little, it'll pass. They've been threatening divorce for as long as I've been alive and nothing ever comes of it.''

"And how long is it now that you've been alive?''

He'd eased into that pretty smoothly.

But Carly didn't resent the question. She was secretly flattered by his interest.

"Thirty-two years. You?'' Two could play the same game.

"Thirty-six. Thirty-seven next month.''

"Oh, you're old,'' she teased him, purposely omitting the fact that she, too, would be another year older in only four days.

"What do we *old* people get out of your magic bag?''

"Jam, raspberry chutney or pickled green tomatoes."

"Homemade?"

"I have summers off work, remember? These jars are the end of last year's gardening and canning."

He nodded and gave her a look out of the corner of his eye. "Can't do much gardening or canning when you're out traveling around."

"I think the world will survive without it."

"You never know."

What Carly did know was that he was just giving her a hard time. She opted for ignoring him and went on with what she'd been saying.

"There's also some romance novels in the sack. Minnie Oliver is eighty-six, but she just loves them. She says that no matter how old the heroine is, when she reads those books she's that same age. She says they keep her young. She also says she likes them steamy. The hotter the better."

"Maybe I'll have to keep my eye on her," he said as if the elderly woman might try to seduce him.

"You don't have to worry about Minnie, but I should warn you about Candy Woodbine. She will likely want to tap dance for you and her tap dances look more like tame stripteases—not that she gets down to her Skivvies, but expect some shedding of scarves or sweaters or whatever she can spare."

"Yeah?" Bax asked with mock interest in his tone. "How old is she?"

"Seventy-three, but she's still kickin'—that's

what she'll tell you—and a little charm tossed back at her will tickle her to death.''

''At seventy-three maybe I shouldn't be tickling her to death,'' Bax joked.

''You know what I mean—it'll thrill her.''

''So, I'm not only the doctor, I'm also the marriage counselor and Cary Grant?''

''Something like that,'' Carly said with a little laugh. ''There's also Frank Montoya. He's eighty and he'll bend your ear about the flood of 1929 when his family was stranded on the farmhouse roof, watching their pig float by. Don't cut him off even though the story will go on for a long time or you'll hurt his feelings.''

Bax glanced at her. ''That's important to you, isn't it? With all these people. That I don't hurt their feelings.''

Carly shrugged. ''They're nice people.''

''So are you.''

That made her cheeks heat and she didn't know what to say. So instead she went back to what she'd been talking about. ''Frank loved that pig. Don't be alarmed if he tears up.''

Bax gave her another pointed glance, chuckling kindly at her.

''Oh, and if Benny Mathis wants you to take a look at a problem with one of his animals, humor him. Every symptom he tells you his cow or horse or goat or dog has is really what's going on with him. He just doesn't like to complain for himself.''

''Is that it?''

"There's more people we'll see, but those are just some of the quirks you'll come across."

"Good thing you warned me. I could see myself getting into some real trouble without you."

"I think you'd probably have done all right on your own." She thought he could probably do all right on his own with anything or anyone.

But then maybe she was biased.

The dirt road that led to the Marris farm came into view then. Carly directed Bax to it, and from that moment on she consciously tried to take a back seat to him. At each house they entered from then on she introduced him and did her best to blend into the woodwork.

She wasn't terribly successful because everywhere they went she was well-known and well liked while Bax was the newcomer people were a little shy of.

He didn't seem to mind and included her himself at every opportunity.

Along the way Carly got to see Bax in action, and it only confirmed her earlier opinion that her father would have approved of this man who had taken over the care of the people who had meant so much to him.

If there was such a thing as a born country doctor, Bax was it.

There was no pretension, no arrogance, no talking over anyone's head. He blended just the right amount of socializing with the practice of medicine, and not even Cary Grant could have charmed everyone more adeptly.

Carly didn't think there was a single home he left without having won over the folks inside. To the point where she felt confident that the next time he made the rounds to the outlying farms and ranches he'd be welcome not only for the gifts and tokens he made note to return with, but also just for being himself.

And Carly realized as they wrapped up the final visit of the day that she felt a little jealous again.

Jealous of the fact that Bax was only beginning these visits while they were likely the last she'd ever make.

Not that it mattered enough to stay in Elk Creek, of course.

But still, she fought a twinge of regret she hadn't anticipated.

Regret that she wouldn't be along on his future visits.

Especially when they seemed to make such a good team.

Chapter Seven

It was after six by the time Carly and Bax made it back to the McDermot ranch.

Since Carly had lived all her life in Elk Creek, she'd known the place when it had been the Martindale ranch—Bax's grandfather Buzz Martindale's spread.

That was long before Buzz's daughter—Bax's mother—had eloped with a man Buzz hadn't approved of. Years of estrangement had finally ended, and when it had Buzz had turned over his house and land to the grown grandchildren he hadn't known before that—Shane, Ry and Bax McDermot and the other brother and sister that Carly had yet to meet.

The original house had been a small farmhouse, but since Shane and Ry had developed a new breed of cow and reaped the success that had come with it, they'd added onto the original home.

So much so that Buzz's old place wasn't much more than the entry to the new, sprawling ranch-style house.

Carly never passed the property without marveling at the addition and that held true as Bax parked in front and helped her from the car.

It was a beautiful place with twin wings gracefully spreading out on either side of the main entrance where separate bedroom suites opened onto a wraparound porch.

Bax didn't bother to knock on the front door when they reached it. But then, this was his house, too. He was merely renting hers for the sake of convenience.

He held the door open for her to go in ahead of him, waiting patiently as she maneuvered on the crutches she wished she could throw into Make-out Lake.

"Anybody home?" Bax called once they were inside, standing in the wide-open entryway from which both wings could be accessed on either side. Straight ahead was the living room, then the formal dining room, and then the kitchen out back.

It was from the kitchen that someone answered.

"We're on the patio."

Bax swept an arm out to let Carly know he wanted her to go first, and they made their way through the tastefully decorated living and dining rooms to find Bax's brother, Shane, filling tall glasses with ice and tea.

"''Bout time you got back,'' Shane greeted them in a tone that took the complaint out of his words. "We're eatin' outside tonight. Barbecuing. That's where everybody is already. Want tea or soda pop or a beer?''

Bax looked to Carly.

"Tea would be good,'' she added.

"Tea for me, too,'' Bax added.

Shane handed two of the glasses he'd filled to Bax, took two more and led the way through the French doors onto the bricked patio where thickly cushioned lawn furniture was occupied by Shane's twin brother, Ry, Shane's wife, Maya, Ry's soon-to-be wife, Tallie, and Buzz.

"Daddy!'' Evie Lee shouted when she spotted Bax before anyone else had even noticed that Shane hadn't returned alone.

"Evie!'' Bax answered, echoing his daughter's enthusiasm as everyone said hello.

The little girl left a cardboard crate full of kittens to charge her father. "I been swimmin' and everything today!'' she announced, going on to give a recounting of an active afternoon.

"…and when the kittens get a little bit older I can have one. Or two or the whole box!'' she finished, clearly repeating what someone had said in answer to whether or not she could have a kitten.

"I don't know about that,'' Bax hedged. "We might just have to visit them here. Our lease may not let us have pets,'' he said with a wink at Carly.

"Uncle Ry and Uncle Shane got you a present. A whole horse!'' Evie Lee added as Bax led Carly to a chair at the big round table where everyone was sitting.

When Carly had shucked the crutches to sit down, Bax took the seat beside her.

"Is that so? A whole horse, huh?" he responded to his daughter's statement, but cast a quizzical look at his two brothers.

They were both giving that same devilish grin Carly had seen on Bax's face, stamping them all brothers.

"He's a buckin' bronco," Evie Lee said. "See him? Over in that place next to the barn? He's soooo pretty and he looks nice but Uncle Ry says he's not as nice as he looks. But they brought him in from bein' wild just for you."

"Gee, thanks," Bax answered facetiously.

"There was a time when this daddy of yours was the best of us all at ridin' a horse like that. Isn't that so, Ry?" Shane said.

"True enough," Ry confirmed.

"Bet it isn't true anymore, though," Shane added, obviously goading Bax. "Not now that he's a big-time *doctor* and all citified. Probably doesn't even remember how to ride a horse at all, let alone one that's tryin' to buck 'im off."

"Bet you're right," Ry agreed again.

"Could you still do it, Daddy?" Evie Lee asked, picking up the gauntlet her uncles had thrown down.

Bax grinned the grin of a confident man. "Probably could."

"*Probably* could? Or *could?*" Shane prodded.

"Never know," Bax answered.

"Not unless we get your rear end up on his back to see."

Carly looked at the sleek black stallion across the yard. Evie Lee was right, it was a beautiful animal. But Carly had been around these parts long enough to know that no matter how docile a wild horse might appear to be, trying to ride it would bring out the worst in it.

"It's been a busy day," she interjected as if that nullified the idea, because the thought of Bax anywhere near the stallion made her uneasy. Even though she knew it was none of her business and she had no right to be nervous. Or to say anything at all.

But it was that pointed comment from her that Bax seemed to hone in on more than any of his brothers' baiting.

"You don't think I can do it, do you?" he asked in a quiet voice for her ears alone.

"I can't imagine why you'd want to."

"It's a pretty good rush," he said by way of explanation. But the lazy smile that stretched his lips as he looked at her made her think that he knew how his riding the horse would unnerve her and was just ornery enough to do it to get a rise out of her.

But Carly was just ornery enough not to let it get a rise out of her.

Or at least not to show it.

Instead, she merely arched an eyebrow at him.

Unfortunately he seemed to interpret that as a challenge.

He set his glass on the table and stood. "Get me

a pair of gloves and some chaps so I don't ruin my pants," he ordered as if they were instruments he needed to perform a surgical procedure.

"Eee-haw!" Buzz hooted, getting into the spirit of things.

"Stay on 'im the regulation eight seconds and we'll do the saddle breakin' for you," Ry said as if setting the terms of a bet.

"But let 'im throw you before that and you come out here to do it yourself," Shane added.

"Deal," Bax answered.

Then he threw Carly another wink. "Good thing we have crutches handy, just in case."

"You can't do much good as the town doctor if you're laid up," she told him.

"Careful or I'm gonna take that as an invitation," he said, purposely misinterpreting her words.

"Come on, if you're gonna do this thing, do this thing," Shane urged and the three brothers headed for the barn.

"I want to see this!" Evie Lee announced, following behind.

"Sometimes I think there's just too big a streak of boy in every man," Tallie said.

"Mmm," Maya agreed while Buzz merely chuckled and got up into the walker he'd needed to get around since breaking his knee several weeks before.

"Guess we all better go out there," Tallie said as the older man made slow progress across the yard. "We may have to pick up the pieces. Can you make it all right, Carly?"

Carly assured her she could, and the women headed for the paddock where the unsuspecting horse waited.

It wasn't long before Ry, Shane and Evie Lee joined them and Buzz at the paddock rails while Bax came out through the barn's side door directly into the enclosed area with the horse.

Carly had wondered why Ry was carrying Bax's white shirt, but when she spotted Bax she understood.

His khaki jeans were covered with the leather chaps he'd requested, his hands were protected by fingerless gloves strapped tight around his thick wrists, and he'd traded his own shirt for a ragged chambray one.

He looked every inch the cowboy with leather reins slung over one shoulder as he approached the stallion, talking softly to it, soothingly.

The animal raised its head from where it had been peacefully munching grass to watch Bax, but it didn't shy away. It stood its ground almost as if it were curious as to what the human had in mind, but showing no fear.

"We used to say that Bax thought like a horse," Shane said to the spectators in general.

But that didn't put rest to any of Carly's tension. She just hoped Bax knew what he was doing.

Although she had to admit he seemed to.

He had sugar cubes in his left hand and when he got close enough to the horse he held one out for him. The animal nibbled it out of his palm, keeping a wary eye on him the whole while.

The treat bought Bax permission to go a few steps nearer until he could feed the stallion the cubes with the animal's nose nearly up against his chest. He kept on murmuring something Carly couldn't hear, but she imagined his deep voice saying endearments and she thought if she were the horse, that in itself might be enough to tame her.

But rather than endearments, she realized he was probably making friends with the animal the way she'd watched him make friends with his patients all afternoon. Charming him. Gaining his trust.

And when he had, he hooked the reins through the driving bit of the bridle and eased them over the stallion's ears.

Carly knew it was probably a feeble hope, but she couldn't help thinking that maybe the horse would just let Bax ride him as Bax stepped around to his side.

Bax smoothed the animal's hind quarter and kept on talking to him as he wrapped the reins around one hand. Then he grabbed hold of the mane with the other and swung a leg up over the horse's back in one smooth, lithe motion.

For a split second the horse just stood there.

But then the fact that he had a rider registered and he took off like a shot, racing several yards, stopping cold, rearing to kick his front legs in midair, lowering them so he could buck with his hind legs, then taking off again to repeat the process. Again and again.

Never had Carly seen an animal as determined as that one to rid itself of a rider.

But Bax didn't merely hang on for dear life, he rode the horse, staying with it, absorbing the shock of each buck, each rearing up that made the animal seem like a giant to Carly.

Beside her, Ry went from observing the event to checking his wristwatch, but for Carly it was an endless eight seconds.

Her heart pounded in her chest and it was as if every jolt of the animal jarred her, too.

Yet even as afraid as she was for Bax's safety, she had to admire what she saw. The way he handled the animal was an impressive sight. His power and strength met that of the beast and he came out the victor when Ry finally yelled, "Time!"

And then, with all the adeptness of a stuntman, Bax actually managed to leap from the bucking bronco's back and land on his feet in a run that took him away from the still-rearing animal.

Buzz and the other McDermot men hooted and hollered and cheered for him, and he faced it with a grin that said he'd enjoyed every second of the ride.

He folded one arm across his waist and took a bow. Then he came to the rail to climb the first rung and swing himself over the top to again land on his feet amid backslaps from his family.

Evie Lee was jumping up and down, clapping her hands and parroting her uncles' and great-grandfather's cheers, but Bax's gaze sought out Carly.

His eyes locked on hers for a moment, beaming

with pride and pleasure, and for that brief time it seemed as if they were the only two people there.

And, Lord, how she wished it were true...

Then he pulled off the gloves and handed them to Shane, unfastened the chaps to slip them off and before Carly knew it, he'd also shed the work shirt and was reaching for his white one from his brother.

It took her so unawares that she didn't have time to brace herself before she was confronted with his naked torso the way she had been on Sunday when she'd caught him coming out of the shower.

Only this time she was having even more difficulty tearing her gaze away from shoulders and biceps that were all tight flesh over hard muscles— not what any doctor acquired in the course of his duties.

The span of his chest was daunting and delectable at once, and Carly's mouth went suddenly dry as her eyes stuck on the slight smattering of hair there, at the vision of brown male nibs, at the six-pack of taut abdominal muscles down his middle to the sexiest navel she'd ever seen peeking from above a pair of jeans.

The whole picture took her breath away and made her head reel as much as if she'd been on that wild horse herself. Her hands ached to be pressed to him, to learn for herself if his skin was as smooth as it looked. As warm. As wonderful...

Then on went the white shirt, blocking her view and, somewhat belatedly, Carly realized that someone had suggested the steaks be put on the grill. Ry had left to take the reins off the stallion and the group was moving back toward the house, leaving Carly and Bax alone.

The silence around them as Bax buttoned his shirt and jammed the tails into his waistband seemed to Carly to shout of her attraction to the man, so she swallowed hard and fought to find her voice.

"I guess you are good at wild horse riding," she said.

He smiled a quirky kind of smile that raised only one corner of his mouth. "Just showin' off," he admitted. "I've had a lot of experience from my misspent youth. I was always the one crazy enough to do the bronc bustin'. I guess once you get the feel for it, you never lose it."

Carly understood having the feel for something.

Or maybe it was having the desire to feel something that she really understood....

"Well, don't do it again," she heard herself blurt out.

Bax laughed. "Yes, ma'am," he said as if accepting a command. Then his tone turned satisfied. "Had you all riled up, did I?"

Riled up. Aroused. Hard to tell the difference if there was one.

"It isn't that you scared me or anything," she denied to save face. "It's just that Elk Creek needs its doctor in one piece."

"I suppose that's true enough. But think of it this way—I only had to spend eight seconds up there. Now my brothers have to do the actual saddle breaking. So I came out ahead and so did Elk Creek."

"Still..."

He leaned over to whisper in her ear much the way he'd whispered to the horse. "Careful or I'm gonna start thinkin' you care."

"I do care. For the town's sake. For Evie Lee's sake."

"And for your sake?"

"I just don't want to share my crutches," she claimed with her nose in the air.

"There's a lot of things I'd like to share with you, but crutches aren't one of them," he said with a bad-boy grin and an unmistakably lascivious glint in his eyes.

Ry came out of the barn just then, having retrieved the reins and put them away.

"Well come on, you two, looks like we're finally eatin'."

Bax did a courtly sweep of his arm. "After you," he said to Carly in a bedroom voice that turned her blood to molten lava.

But she merely shook her head as if she'd just suffered a silly joke and headed for the house again.

Matters weren't helped, though, when Bax fell into step beside her and put a hand at the small of her back.

As always his touch spread a heat all its own, lighting a fire to the already molten lava.

Carly and Bax didn't have another moment to themselves the rest of the evening. At least not until they left the ranch.

Evie Lee had fallen asleep before dessert was served and had been put to bed with an assurance that one of her uncles would take her home in the morning. That left Carly and Bax alone in the car on the way home.

The temperature hadn't cooled much with the setting sun so all the windows were rolled down to let the air flow through. Carly was grateful for that. It helped diffuse some of the intimacy of being in the dark car with him.

"Tomorrow's the meet-and-greet reception," he said, disrupting the quiet hum of the motor as he drove.

"That's right. I'd forgotten about it. I didn't expect to be here."

"But since you are, would you charge me extra for comin' to it with me? I already owe you for introducing me to everyone and giving me the briefing about them beforehand."

Carly had laid her head against the seat back and she kept it there even as she turned to look at him. "I didn't know I was charging you for today."

"You could. For being my consultant. Except that the service you provided was priceless."

There was an edge of teasing to his tone, and his dimple was showing in the cheek that she could see.

For a moment Carly lost herself in the sight of his profile. It was as well-chiseled as the front view, and she got lost in the sharp jawline for a moment before she recalled that they were having a conversation.

"The reception is in the evening, isn't it?" she asked to pull her thoughts back into order.

"At six. In the church basement so folks aren't

coming to the office and expecting me to work. I'd really appreciate it if you'd come with me.''

Not just be there, go *with* him.

''I think I can do that,'' she said, despite the warning alarm in her head that told her she should refuse. That he didn't really *need* her there. That they were spending too much time together. That she was liking him much too much...

But the agreement was already given and she couldn't take it back.

''Great!'' Bax said in response to her acceptance. ''Now I'll be lookin' forward to it.''

''Weren't you before?''

''You know how those things are—you have to be center stage the whole time. Makes me uncomfortable.''

''A lot of people would like being center stage. It would be a big ego boost for them.''

''I'm more of a hands-on guy myself,'' he said with a sideways glance at her to go with the innuendo.

''Mmm,'' was all Carly answered, thinking that his hands on her had definite appeal.

Not that she'd ever say it.

They'd reached Elk Creek by then. It was after ten o'clock, all was quiet and it suddenly seemed to Carly that she'd gotten her earlier wish—it truly felt as if they were the only two people in the world.

And she was liking *that* too much, too.

Bax pulled into the driveway in front of her house, stopped the engine and wasted no time getting out. He came around to her side to open the door and held her crutches for her as she got out.

"Want to trade houses for the night?" he asked then.

"Trade houses?"

"It just occurred to me that without Evie Lee at home I could sleep in the guest cottage and you could have a night in your own bed if you wanted," he explained as they went onto the porch and in the front door.

"That's okay. I'm all set up in the cottage and you're settled into the house. Besides, I don't mind. I've always liked the bed out there."

For the first time in her life the mention of *bed* felt wicked. Titillatingly wicked.

Maybe because the moment she'd said the word she'd realized that within a short time that was where they'd both be—in their respective beds. But what had popped into her mind was the image of Bax in her bed in the cottage rather than in the one he was using upstairs.

In her bed in the cottage with the sheets dropped low enough to bare the naked chest she'd seen earlier.

In her bed in the cottage with the sheets dropped low enough to bare the naked chest she'd seen earlier and her in bed beside him...

Carly tried to push the instant fantasy into oblivion, but it was stubborn and she ended up deciding the best thing to do was to end this evening and get a safe distance from the man who was provoking the unwelcome thoughts.

So she didn't pause inside but instead headed straight for the back door.

Unfortunately Bax went with her to hold open that door. Then he went out into the breezeway and across to the cottage with her, as well.

And there she was at the cottage door, with Bax in the soft glow of the motion detector light that had turned on as they'd come outside.

She had to take a good, hard look at his white shirt to force herself to remember that he was, in fact, fully clothed or she didn't think she could keep herself from falling into his arms. On purpose.

"Thanks for everything you did today," he was saying when she yanked herself back into reality.

"Don't think anything about it. I enjoyed myself. It was good to see all those people before I left." And she *was* going to leave, she reminded herself firmly. Soon. And nothing was going to get in her way this time. Not even a man who stared down at her with sea-foam eyes that delved into her soul and turned her insides to mush.

Not even a man whose lips she suddenly recalled the feel of much too vividly...

"Before you leave," he repeated, more to himself than to her, as if he were reminding himself the way she'd just reminded herself.

But if he'd intended that reminder the way she'd intended hers—as a caution that whatever was happening between them had no future—it didn't appear to help.

Because he remained standing there, studying her face, smiling at whatever it was he saw there.

"We should probably call it a night," Carly said then, trying to hang on to her resistance but hearing the words come out in a voice that was nearly breathless and far more sensual sounding than she'd intended.

"Probably should," he agreed in a raspy tone of his own.

But he didn't move from that spot where he stood close in front of her. So close she could see every long eyelash that shaded his eyes.

So close she could feel the heat of his big body.

So close she could have arched her back and her breasts would have touched his chest...

"And I probably shouldn't, but I'm gonna kiss you good-night again," he added then.

His low, deep voice and the sight of those handsome features put together in such rugged perfection mesmerized her. The only thing Carly could think to say was, "Probably shouldn't," in a way that sounded more inviting than anything else.

"Probably shouldn't," he agreed just before he lowered his mouth to hers.

But tonight the kiss he gave her was not merely a brief peck. Tonight it was a full-blown, genuine kiss with lips that knew just the right amount of pressure, just the right amount of persuasion to entice her lips to part slightly to match his, to give as good as she got.

Tonight it was a kiss that drew her in. That rocked her.

That left her knowing somewhere deep inside that things would somehow never be the same again.

And then it was over.

Bax straightened away from her. He captured her eyes with his once more and she could tell she wasn't the only one of them to have felt the earth shake.

"Probably shouldn't have," he whispered, as if talking to himself.

But the fact remained that he had.

They had.

And as Carly said good-night and went into the cottage, all she could think was that she wanted more.

No matter what it put into jeopardy.

Chapter Eight

"Boy-oh-boy, do they get up early over at that place," Evie Lee announced the following morning at the breakfast table.

Bax was still slightly bleary-eyed. Shane had called at five-thirty to tell him Evie Lee was ready to come home, and here it was 6:07 and she was eating a bowl of cereal and chattering with vigor when he could usually count on her staying in bed until seven.

And since Bax had had some trouble falling asleep the night before, it wasn't easy keeping up with her.

"They gots a rooster," Evie Lee continued, "that makes lots of noise and it waked me up. Not like the cock-a-doodle-doo noise in the cartoons. It makes a worser noise than that.''

Bax smiled at his daughter's inexperience with country life. But then for the six years she'd been alive he'd been practicing medicine in Denver and there wasn't a rooster crowing at dawn in a high-rise apartment building. This was just the kind of thing he'd come to Elk Creek for—so Evie Lee would have a taste of what he considered real life. The kind of life he'd known growing up.

Just then Evie Lee hopped off the chair and headed for the back door. "I wanna go tell Carly what the kitties did this morning.''

"Whoa, hold on there,'' Bax said in a hurry, stopping her just short of charging out. "It's too early to go bargin' in on Carly.''

"But she said it was okay for me to visit her anytime.''

"Not at six in the morning. She's probably not even up yet.''

"Then I'll wake her up,'' the little girl said reasonably. "I'll make the rooster sound for her.''

"Uh-uh.'' Bax gave his daughter a firm stare and wiggled a hooked index finger, motioning her to come back to the table.

"But I *like* Carly,'' Evie Lee moaned.

"I like Carly, too, but that doesn't mean we can disturb her.'' Even though she was disturbing the holy hell out of him and his sleep patterns. He couldn't stop thinking about her long enough to get any rest.

But that was his own fault.

Evie Lee dragged her feet back to the kitchen table and climbed onto her chair to take another bite of cereal. And just that fast her pique changed to a new interest.

"You like Carly, too?" she asked.

"She seems nice," Bax said, downplaying the truth.

Because the truth was that he liked her a lot. Enough to have been up until the wee hours of the morning thinking about her. Picturing what she might be doing out in the cottage. Calculating how much distance separated them. Wondering what would happen if he crossed that distance and appeared on her doorstep. Imagining himself finding her in some slinky, low-cut little nightgown, her hair hanging loose and free and silky around her shoulders, her face all pink and pretty from a fresh scrubbing, her topaz eyes wide with surprise but her rosebud mouth smiling a welcome. That same rosebud mouth he'd kissed twice now. And was dying to kiss again. And again. And again. Before they moved on to so much more...

"Do you like her for a girlfriend?" Evie Lee asked, interrupting his wandering thoughts.

"She's just a nice person," he hedged, uncomfortable with his daughter's probing into something he wished wasn't happening at all.

"I heard the big grandad say you mittened her."

Bax had to think a minute to figure out what that statement meant. He knew the *big grandad* was Buzz. That was Evie Lee's version of great-grandfather. But it took him a moment to figure out why Buzz would say anything about Bax, Carly and mittens.

Then it occurred to him.

"You mean *smitten?*"

"Okay. But you don't have any smittens, do you? I never saw you put any on Carly."

Bax laughed lightly. "*Smitten* isn't the same as *mittens.* It means *like,* too."

"Oh. Then the big grandad thinks you like Carly. A whole bunch."

Bax just took a drink of his coffee rather than commenting on that.

"Do you like her like you liked Alisha?"

There was a note of caution in Evie Lee's voice even now when she said the other woman's name.

Not that Bax didn't understand it. Alisha had been both their nightmares.

What he couldn't tell was if Evie Lee was asking that question because she was concerned he might repeat with Carly the mistake he'd made in his second marriage.

And it wrenched his heart to think his daughter might have those concerns. That part of his past was something he'd regret and feel guilty for having put Evie Lee through for as long as he lived, but he hoped she could put it behind her.

"You don't have to worry about my bringing home any more stepmothers, Evie," he assured her quietly.

"I wasn't worryin' about *that,*" she said. "I was just wondering if you like Carly. I like her and I think she likes me."

"I think she likes you, too."

"Alisha pretended she liked me at first but she didn't."

Another wrench of his heart—to know that this little girl carried with her the knowledge that her former stepmother hadn't liked her.

"There wasn't anything wrong with you, you know? Alisha was just not a nice person and she fooled us both. She was who deserved not to be liked. Not you."

"But Carly *is* a nice person."

That was a statement without any trace of uncertainty in Evie Lee's voice. It was something Bax was grateful for. If he and Evie Lee were going to be in such close proximity to Carly even for just a short while, he was glad Carly was so patient and friendly toward his daughter.

"Yes, I think Carly is a nice person, that's why I said it."

"And I think she really likes me, not just pretends, because she laughs at my jokes and she has a good time playin' the Candy Land game with me and she even gived me a hug the other day when I said something she thought was cute. Alisha never did that."

"I think Carly really does like you, too."

"Then I think it's okay if she was your girl-friend."

Bax chuckled again. "Thank you for your permission," he joked.

"You're welcome," Evie Lee answered seriously. "If I can't go see Carly, then I'm gonna watch cartoons till I can."

"All right."

Evie Lee hopped down from the chair for the second time and Bax watched her do a sedate skip through the swinging door, aching with love for her. Aching for the pain he'd caused her by bringing Alisha into her life.

Never again, he vowed for the hundredth time since his second marriage had ended.

Never again would he let a woman like Alisha anywhere near his daughter.

And once more he thanked his lucky stars that Carly seemed genuinely fond of Evie Lee. That she didn't appear to mind having Evie Lee around since Evie Lee enjoyed Carly's company so much.

"Like father, like daughter," Bax muttered to himself, sliding low in his seat so his head could rest on the back of the chair and he could catch forty winks.

But napping came no easier than full-blown sleeping had the night before.

Instead he was thinking about just how much *he* enjoyed Carly's company. More than he'd enjoyed any woman's company in a long, long time.

They seemed to be such a great fit.

He liked talking to her. Listening to her. She was so down to earth. So uncomplicated. So sweet-natured. So accepting. So kind. So funny. So thoughtful.

She had a touch of naiveté about her that was a breath of fresh air to him after Alisha. Being a small-town doctor's daughter gave Carly a certain amount of built-in status, yet she didn't seem to know that. She didn't seem to realize how well thought of she was. Or if she did, she took it all in stride because he hadn't seen any signs of it inflating her ego.

He couldn't think of anyone better to tell him about the townsfolk. She had a way of giving him insight into his patients, into their strengths and weaknesses, all the while making them sound so amusing, so interesting, so human and likable, that he ended up seeing them as whole, three-dimensional people before he even met them.

And as for what she was doing with Evie Lee, he couldn't put a price on the gift she was giving his daughter. Carly was letting Evie Lee feel that she was a likable little girl again, rebuilding the self-esteem Alisha had damaged.

He was crazy about the way Carly looked, too. Not only was she beautiful, but it was as if her warmth, her intelligence, her humor were all reflected in her face to give it a deeper kind of beauty than Alisha had had. And he sure as hell couldn't get the picture of her out of his mind, he liked it so much. Head to toe, she was perfect. Shiny hair. Adorable face. A body he was itching to know more of...

Okay, so he was hot for her along with everything else. No sense denying it.

Hotter for her than he'd been for anyone since his first wife. Definitely hotter than he'd been for Alisha even though she'd been incredibly gorgeous. Hotter than he had thought he'd ever be for anyone again.

Carly had an under-the-surface, beguiling sort of sexiness that left him consumed with wanting to know if her skin was as satiny as it looked. With wanting to trace every inch of her body with his fingertips. With wanting to feel her pressed so close to him, he didn't know where he ended and she began. With wanting to fill his hands with those small breasts. With wanting to bury his face in her hair, in the soft side of her neck. With wanting to bury himself inside her.

He just plain wanted her. So bad, it was something that seemed to emanate from the marrow of his bones.

And he didn't know how to shake it.

If only he could find just one fault, he thought. One thing that would turn him off.

But he couldn't. No matter how hard he tried.

And he did try.

Then just one fault occurred to him. Not a flaw in Carly herself, but a fault in what came with her— she was leaving town.

And *that* was a negative. A great big fat negative.

Or was it? a voice in the back of his head asked.

Bax opened his eyes and gave up trying to nap. Instead he stared at the ceiling, looking at things from a different perspective suddenly.

Maybe the fact that Carly was hell-bent on leaving town was a positive thing.

He wasn't ready to jump into another serious relationship. In fact, he'd come to Elk Creek with every intention of avoiding it. But what about a not-serious, short-term relationship? With a genuinely good person? Wasn't that something else entirely?

It was.

It was also something that might work out pretty well, now that he thought about it.

What was wrong with a brief encounter with a woman who made him feel terrific again? Who made his daughter feel terrific again?

Both he and Evie Lee knew Carly was leaving before long. And didn't that knowledge give them a sort of armor that would keep them from getting dangerously close to her? Didn't the fact that she wouldn't be around for long make getting too close impossible? Wouldn't it keep either of them from becoming attached to Carly?

And knowing that, why couldn't they have fun with her while she was around? What harm would there be as long as he kept in mind that this was only a temporary situation? As long as he reminded Evie Lee of it?

He took a minute to analyze everything, but even after he had he couldn't come up with any harm that would be caused or any reason why he and Evie Lee couldn't have this time with Carly. She was starting him off on the right foot with his future patients. She was making this transition in both his life and that of his daughter pleasant and easy. Why shouldn't those benefits be embraced and appreciated and reveled in? Why should he be fighting it?

Okay, so maybe the attraction he had for her threw a curve into things. But if he made sure to foster no illusions about her being around forever, about any chance of a long-term, serious relationship, why couldn't he and Evie Lee enjoy her company? So long as he knew the score he couldn't get hurt, could he?

He didn't think so.

And he didn't think Evie Lee would get hurt, either, because she knew as well as he did that Carly was leaving, that this whole arrangement had a limit to it.

So maybe he could relax a little and just enjoy what was going on between him and Carly.

He just had to keep the reins of his emotions in hand so that if they started to run too wild he could pull them back into control.

But unless that happened he couldn't see any reason not to let the reins go slack, not to ride this out until it came to its natural conclusion. He couldn't see any reason to go on fretting over it.

So he wasn't going to.

What he *was* going to do was let himself indulge a little. Let himself relax. Let himself relish what time he did have with her.

And then, when the day came for her to leave, he'd kiss her goodbye and watch her set off on that trip of hers. No different than sending a friend off on a vacation.

Except that what he was feeling for Carly was a lot more than simple friendship.

And suddenly the thought of kissing her goodbye and watching her set off on her own brought an odd twinge to his gut that told him that even though he'd just talked himself into all the reasons her not sticking around indefinitely was a positive thing, he was having some trouble keeping it in mind.

But still, that was the reality of their situation. She was here now and she'd be gone before long.

So while she was here, he'd enjoy it. Enjoy her.

And when it was over?

She would have left him with a good footing in the community and a daughter who felt better about herself.

"And maybe with a heart that's a little broken," he muttered to himself as if someone else were injecting another viewpoint.

But even if that ended up being the case, he'd just deal with it. After all, he'd lived through losing his wife and the mother of his child to an early, unexpected death.

He'd lived through an ugly divorce.

He could live through putting Carly on a train and watching her leave after only a few days of knowing her.

Couldn't he?

Sure he could.

He just had to make sure he didn't lose sight of the fact that she was going.

But then, it wasn't something he thought he was likely to forget.

Carly had spent the day with her sister, helping out where she could with the new baby and Hope's other three kids.

She'd left home early, making her way on the crutches from the cottage, down the path that led to the medical building and around the corner to Hope's house. Because she'd gone out that back way, without going into the kitchen in the main house first, she hadn't seen either Bax or Evie Lee all day.

As she took a second shower and shampooed her hair late that afternoon, she tried not to think about how much she'd missed them both.

How could that be? she asked herself.

She barely knew either of them and yet a few hours apart had left her dying to be with them again, wondering what they'd done today, feeling that no matter what they'd done, she was sorry not to have done it with them.

Lately she was beginning to think she'd lost her mind.

What possible difference could it make to her *what* they'd done without her? Or if they'd missed her, too—which was the other thing on her mind.

And yet there it was—it did make a difference to her.

It was all probably due to the fact that Bax was new in town, she reasoned. He was someone she didn't know the way she knew everyone else in Elk Creek. And the unknown was always more interesting, more intriguing than the known.

That was all there was to it.

That was probably even why she'd caught her mind wandering to Bax all day long. Why she'd had such trouble concentrating on anything anyone said to her while visions of his sharply planed features danced through her head. While images of those broad shoulders, that well-muscled chest, that hard, flat belly swam before her eyes. While memories of his lips on hers made her turn to jelly...

She scrubbed her scalp extra hard, then rinsed her hair, trying to wash away those very same thoughts right then.

"It's just the novelty," she said, as if saying it aloud would make it more convincing.

Because she wanted to be convinced.

She *didn't* want to be racked with thoughts of the man, with this sense of loss for having not spent a few hours with him. It was only a matter of days until she left Elk Creek, and if she felt this way now, what was going to happen to her then?

It was just dumb, she told herself sternly as she turned off the water and reached outside the shower door for her towel.

The whole thing was dumb.

Lying in her bed last night reliving that good-night kiss again and again. Closing her eyes and pretending he was there with her, kissing her once more. More than kissing her. Dreaming about him when she did finally fall asleep. Waking with him in her thoughts first thing in the morning. Fantasizing about him all the while she should have been listening to her sister and her nephews and the other people who'd come to visit.

It was all dumb. Dumber than dumb.

"So stop it," she commanded herself. "He's just another guy."

Except that didn't ring true even out loud.

Bax wasn't just another guy.

He was a guy whose eyes could melt her insides with a glance. He was a guy who had a way about him that made her forget everything else when she was with him. He was a guy whose smile lit a fire in her blood.

Why couldn't she have met him before? Before his Peace Corps days. Before he'd married. Before he'd developed ties that bound him. When they could have seen the world together.

Better late than never… a little voice in her head said.

But she didn't necessarily agree with that.

What was good about meeting him now?

On the other hand, it suddenly occurred to her that maybe a little time with him now, before she left, was better than no time with him at all.

That gave her pause. Or maybe the appeal of that idea was what gave her pause.

But either way, it left her thinking about what she'd been telling herself the whole day—basically to put as much distance as she could between them, to refuse to do things like this meet-and-greet with him, to avoid him.

But what if instead of that—which she obviously wasn't pulling off anyway since she was getting ready for the meet-and-greet, after all—she just gave in to the urge to spend time with him now, while she could?

Because really, what was the worst that could happen? she asked herself as she left the bathroom and limped to where she had a brand-new pale-blue summer dress waiting for her on the bed.

The worst that could happen was that when she left in a few days she'd miss him and Evie Lee the way she had today. And that wasn't too horrible.

Okay, so the hours had seemed to drag. So she hadn't enjoyed herself much, or enjoyed any of the other people she'd been with. So she'd watched the clock and counted every minute that passed until she could be with Bax again.

But when she was finally off on her trip, when she was in the middle of someplace new, meeting more new people, wouldn't she be so completely engulfed in the experience that she wouldn't even think about Bax?

It seemed so to her.

And if she felt a little of what she'd felt today? She'd call it homesickness and wait for it to pass. Because surely it would.

Wouldn't it?

It would just have to, that was all there was to it.

And in the meantime, she could have the memory of these days spent with him to carry with her. To relive in her mind on long plane rides, at lonely moments, lying in bed in some strange place.

She could consider meeting Bax now as just the beginning of her adventure. Someone new to get to know the way she'd meet new people in her travels and want to get to know them.

That didn't seem so unreasonable.

"Or maybe it's just an excuse," she muttered to herself.

But excuse or no excuse, she knew spending time with him was what she was going to end up doing one way or another, so she might as well put the best spin on it that she could. And the best spin she could think of was that Bax coming to town now was just an opportunity to practice dealing with someone she hadn't known her whole life. To work on a skill she'd need when she finally left Elk Creek.

Certainly that spin made her more comfortable than admitting she was giving in to spending time with Bax because she was mind-numbingly attracted to the guy.

She just hoped she wasn't fooling herself.

At least not too much...

Chapter Nine

The meet-and-greet should have been called the meet-and-greet-and-bring-the-new-doctor-a-casserole because so many women came bearing foil pans for Bax and his daughter.

It happened frequently enough that when Bax spotted someone approaching with their offering, he began to whisper his guess as to what kind of casserole it might be.

Of course his guesses got more and more farcical as the evening wore on—cream of outdated encyclopedia pages from Nan Carpenter, who looked like an old-fashioned librarian with her hair in a bun; duck à la dill weed from Maude Benchley, who had a mallard embroidered on her blouse; long drink of watercress custard from Prissy Palicomo, who stood a full six feet tall.

It was all silly but not unkind and his comical conjectures teased Carly at the same time for the descriptions and commentaries she made as sidebars to her own introductions.

Nearly the whole town streamed in and out of the church basement, and what was scheduled to be a two-hour reception stretched until nearly ten o'clock at night. But for Carly the time flew by.

She and Bax stayed together in what was actually a two-person receiving line, which meant it was a concentrated evening of being with him. And even though Carly did what she'd done the day before as they'd visited the outlying farms and ranches—performing the introductions, then trying to fade into the background as Bax got to know the townsfolk—there was still no question that she was with him. That they were sharing the evening. That she was enjoying herself.

When the church basement finally saw the last of the people who'd come to meet Bax, there was a tableful of the casseroles along with cakes, pies and various loaves of banana, zucchini, cranberry and poppy seed breads for him to take home.

Luckily he'd driven his station wagon so that Carly wouldn't have to walk. It gave him a way to get everything home.

By then Carly's ankle was throbbing and since she couldn't help load the goodies into the back of the station wagon anyway, she sat on one of the folding chairs that lined the walls and put her feet up on another.

Evie Lee, who had had a full evening of meeting and playing with just about every child in town, joined Carly to lie down on the chairs beside her, laying her head in Carly's lap.

"Tired?" Carly asked.

"No, not me," Evie Lee claimed as she closed her eyes and fell instantly asleep beneath Carly's hand smoothing her hair.

Carly smiled down at the cherub and then rested her own head against the wall and closed her eyes, too, as Bax and several of the husbands of the Ladies' League members who had given the party and were doing cleanup detail began to make trip after trip to the car.

She lost track of time, but it didn't seem long before Bax's voice interrupted her reverie.

"Looks like my girls have had it," he said when the gifts of food were all loaded and he'd come back for her and Evie Lee.

Carly opened her eyes and smiled at the "my girls" part, feeling a warm flush of pleasure to be included.

"Mmm," was all she answered, continuing to smooth Evie Lee's hair, but looking all the way up the long length of Bax.

He was wearing cowboy boots, a pair of gray corduroy slacks and a dove-gray shirt with a charcoal tie as he stood smiling that secret smile of his.

"Guess I better get you both home," he said then.

He bent over and scooped his daughter into his

arms, and the sight of the small child held against her father's broad, capable chest warmed Carly, too.

"Want me to come back and carry you out?" he offered, only half teasing. "I'm betting you've been on that ankle of yours too long tonight."

"It's putting up a little fuss, but I'm fine," she said as she retrieved her crutches from the floor in front of the chairs and got up onto them again.

But the flinch that escaped then wasn't from the pain in her ankle, it was from the rawness under her arms left by too many hours on the crutches.

Bax seemed to know that. "Even pads don't help those arm pieces after a while, do they?"

"Sounds like you know from experience."

"A little. Broke my leg when I was a teenager and did my time on them. They're murder."

"You can say that again."

He didn't, though. Instead, they both called a quick good-night to the cleanup crew and made their way out of the church basement.

The cooler, fresh air outside felt like heaven to Carly and she took several deep breaths of it as Bax laid Evie Lee on the back seat and maneuvered a seat belt around her. Then he helped Carly into the passenger side and they went the short distance home.

Once they got there Bax backed into the driveway and turned off the engine. But before he made a move to get out from behind the wheel he turned to Carly. "I want to take a look at your ankle. How about if I put Evie Lee in bed, set up the footbath and you can soak in it while I get all this stuff out of the car?''

''Okay,'' Carly agreed. She didn't need a lot of persuading because not only did the foot soaking sound good, so did the thought of prolonging the evening with Bax and honing those getting-to-know-you skills she'd talked herself into as she'd dressed for this evening.

In the time it took Carly to get into the house and unwrap her ankle, Bax had his daughter in bed and was ready with the footbath in the living room so Carly could sit comfortably on the couch to use it.

She felt a little guilty for not being able to help him carry in the food, but that didn't keep her from watching him as he did. In fact, she was a rapt audience, memorizing every detail.

There was a slight, unconscious swagger to the way he walked. It came more from being a little bowlegged than from ego, but it was so sexy it made her mouth water.

He kept his back straight, not hunching even as he carried casseroles stacked from waist to chin, and she couldn't help remembering just how impressive that same back was when it was bare, wishing suddenly that he would chuck the gray shirt and finish the chore that way.

Even from a distance, there was no denying that the man was lethally handsome. So lethally handsome that she wanted that face, that body, his every movement, every nuance, etched into her brain like a mental videotape she could replay again and again when she was far away from there. From him.

But no matter how hard she tried to ingrain his image into her mind, she wasn't sure if her memory would ever do him justice.

It took him nearly half an hour to unload the car and store everything, but then he came back to Carly with a towel flung over one shoulder, carrying a plate filled with slices of various sweet breads and two glasses of iced tea. He set the goodies and drinks on the coffee table and then sat beside her on the sofa, pulling the towel from his shoulder.

"How are we doing?" he asked.

"Better," Carly answered, knowing he meant her ankle. But her answer included more than that because her ankle wasn't the only thing to improve with his arrival.

"Let's have a look," he ordered, bending over to make a sling out of the towel and catching her foot in it as she raised it from the water.

Then he took hold of her leg and swung her so she was sitting crossways on the couch with her foot in his lap so he could pat it dry and study her injury.

Carly reached down to remove the strappy sandal she wore on her other foot so she didn't soil the sofa and was grateful for the fact that her dress was long and the skirt full enough to stay draped around her legs to maintain her modesty.

"Doesn't look like we did too much damage tonight," he said as he examined the foot and ankle. "Swelling's down some. Bruising is right on track. Want me to wrap it again or shall we let it breathe a little?"

"Let it breathe. I'll wrap it again before I go to sleep."

"Okay." He tossed the towel to the floor and sat back, keeping hold of her foot to do a gentle massage of her toes. "Does this hurt?"

"No. It feels good." Great, in fact. Wonderful. Warm. Tender. Arousing...

It occurred to her that she should have said it hurt so he'd stop, that she was safer if he didn't touch her.

The trouble was, then he might have actually stopped.

"Did you find a place in the refrigerator for all those casseroles?" she asked instead.

"In the refrigerator, in the freezer on top of the refrigerator and in the big freezer in the laundry room, too. Looks like I won't have to cook for a year."

"At least," Carly agreed.

"It was amazin' to have so many people think of me, though. There aren't too many places where you get treated that well."

Carly hadn't thought of it that way. It was all just part of Elk Creek's customary welcome, a welcome she'd have been a part of had she planned on being here. But seeing it through Bax's eyes, she guessed it was something special.

"Folks here are thoughtful," she said.

"More than I've found in other places. Looks like I made a good choice in this town."

"I think so."

He grinned at her. "Then how come you're leavin' it?"

"Just to see what else is out there. Not because there's anything wrong with the town itself." And she was surprised at how defensive she sounded.

Bax must have picked up on it because he left that subject and went back to the previous one. "Think there's any Engelhart casserole in the bunch."

"Engelhart casserole?"

"It's something my wife—my first wife—used to make. That's what she called it. I don't know if it's a real thing or not. It was a concoction with ground beef and noodles and cheeses and I don't know what all. I just know I liked it and haven't had it since she died. But with that many casseroles I was hoping there might be one Engelhart among them."

"I don't know. I can't say I've ever heard of it or of anybody around here making anything called that," Carly said, wondering if his mentioning his first wife allowed her an opening to pry. Just a little. To soothe her curiosity.

But opening or not, she decided to pry anyway.

"Your first wife was Evie Lee's mom, right?"

"Mm-hmm," he confirmed, seeming more interested in her foot than in anything else.

"What happened to her—if you don't mind my asking?"

"She died about an hour after Evie Lee was born. She had a brain aneurysm on the delivery table."

"Without warning?"

"Not a clue. The pregnancy was normal, healthy.

Labor had seemed fine. No signs of toxemia. And then—boom—she blew a vessel. They had to take Evie Lee cesarean, rush Lee Ann into brain surgery. But they couldn't save her.''

"You must have been devastated."

"To put it mildly."

"And there you were, left with a newborn."

"Left with a newborn and a double-duty job practicing medicine and teaching."

"Did you have help?"

"My sister came to stay. It was a good thing because I knew how to deliver babies, but taking care of them once they were here was not my area of expertise. I had to be walked through it as if I were a baby myself. I guess I learned, but to tell you the truth, I couldn't swear I could do it again. Most of that first year is a blur. I just got through it somehow. Barely."

"And after the first year?"

"My sister had to go back to her own life and I was on my own. It wasn't easy, but we managed. Well, I managed. Evie Lee got shuffled more than she should have. I felt bad about that. Real bad. That's part of why I ended up marryin' again."

"To give Evie Lee a sort-of mom—she told me she'd had a *sort-of mom* named Alisha." Carly thought it was better not to say what else Evie Lee had said about Alisha.

"*Sort-of mom* is a better title than Alisha deserved," he said, his tone much different than it had been when he'd talked about his first wife. Much harsher, much harder.

"Evie Lee didn't seem too fond of her," Carly confessed as a means of prying a bit more.

"Evie Lee didn't like Alisha at all. With good cause."

That seemed to stall things.

Carly took a different tack to keep it going. "How long were you married?"

"Less than a year. She was a nurse—that's how I met her. I didn't have time to be out doing a lot of socializin'. But I worked with Alisha and that made it easier than maybe it should have been to get close to her. We dated some. She was pretty— on the outside, anyway—and I thought we had the same values, the same goals, the same agenda...."

He drifted off for a split second, then came back to finish what he'd been saying.

"She pretended that she loved kids—Evie Lee in particular. One thing led to another."

"You married her."

His hands were still gentle and careful, but there was more pressure in them all of a sudden. A sign, Carly thought, of strong feelings about whatever had happened with his second wife.

"I married her," he said as if it left a sour taste in his mouth. "She quit her job. Said she wanted to be a full-time mom, stay at home with Evie Lee."

"It didn't work out that way?"

"Oh, Alisha wanted to stay home, all right. But not to be with Evie. She wanted to shop and go to fancy lunches and play some kind of social-climbing game. Guess she figured a doctor for a husband—

even a former good ol' Texas boy of a doctor—was the first step."

"What about Evie Lee?"

"Evie Lee tied her down. She interfered with Alisha's agenda." That word again, hit hard and disparagingly. "Evie was four when I married Alisha. Alisha thought it was time for preschool so she sent her there two afternoons a week. That was okay. No harm in it. But that was just the beginning. She looked for any way to get rid of Evie—play groups, baby-sitters, day care, shoving her off on neighbors—anything so she could be free to hobnob."

"And Evie Lee wasn't happy about it."

"Evie Lee wasn't happy, period. She was quiet. Sullen. Fearful. But she didn't say anything against Alisha. I talked to one of the psychiatrists at the hospital. He recommended a child psychiatrist at Children's Hospital in Denver and I went to see him, even brought Evie to see him. He did a workup on her. Said she was having normal adjustment problems to the introduction of a stepmother. Nothing to worry about."

"So you didn't worry."

"I still worried. Kept taking her to the shrink. But I still didn't know what was really going on when I wasn't home."

"How did you find out?"

"I came home one day when Alisha wasn't plannin' on it. She was having a tea party for some women she thought were hot stuff. Apparently Evie was exiled to her room to keep her out of the way. But a tea party was right up Evie's alley. She'd gone into our room, gotten into Alisha's things. Shoes mostly, and lipstick to pretty herself up—''

''And decided to invite herself to the party.'' Carly would have smiled at the thought of the little girl dressing herself up and joining in if the tone of this wasn't so ominous.

''Alisha got furious—something she apparently did a lot when she was alone with Evie—and locked her in a closet. That's where I found Evie. Crying in a closet. Terrified of the dark. Her arm bruised from where Alisha had grabbed her to throw her in it.''

Bax accidentally bent her ankle too much and Carly involuntarily pulled away from his grip.

''Did I hurt you?'' he said, alarmed.

''Just a little. My ankle isn't very flexible.''

''I'm sorry,'' he said effusively, instantly returning to a much softer massage. ''I guess just thinking about this riles me up.''

''What did you do about it?''

''Alisha was out within the hour.''

''And you divorced her.''

''Got a lawyer the next day. And took some serious stock of myself and the life I was leadin'.''

''Which is what led you here to Elk Creek.''

He nodded somberly.

''Evie Lee doesn't seem too much the worse for wear,'' Carly said because it was true and because she wanted to ease some of the guilt she could see he was carrying around.

''There are residual effects. But I'm working on it. Her being around you has seemed to help.''

"Me? I haven't done anything."

"You like her. You treat her well, that means a lot."

And his massage was suddenly deeper, more penetrating. Just the way his green eyes were when they met hers then.

Carly couldn't have pinpointed when exactly a change had taken place. But it had. A change in the air around them.

It was filled with intimacy. And Carly had a new awareness of Bax, a more heightened awareness. Of every tiny detail. Of the way his brow creased to let her know he'd been struck by the same sense of closeness between them. Of the way all his features came together to form a rugged, masculine sort of beauty. Of the way his mouth turned up at the corners even when he wasn't smiling. Of how sharp his jawline was. How thick his neck where it dipped into the collar of his shirt.

She realized only then that somewhere since leaving the church he'd taken off his tie and opened the collar button of his shirt. She could see only a hint of the hair smattering his chest, but it was enough to remind her of the magnificence of that chest. The magnificence that carried through in broad shoulders and incredible biceps and thick forearms and wrists, and those hands that were no longer massaging her foot but now caressing it...

"Evie and I are both a little bit nuts about you," he said in a soft voice that lightened the tone of things.

"Maybe you're just a little bit nuts, period," she

teased him, sounding much more seductive than she'd intended.

"Maybe I am," he agreed with a half grin that dimpled only one cheek. "But Evie Lee is a pretty good judge of people."

Bax held her eyes with his, and even if Carly had wanted to break away she didn't think she could have. Something about the depth of his gaze kept her hypnotized, enthralled, enchanted.

Why did he have to be so great-looking? she wondered. So great-smelling? So great all around...

He reached one hand around to the back of her neck then to guide her forward, nearer to him, as he leaned to the side enough to meet her.

There was no question that he was going to kiss her, and Carly's pulse went into overdrive, beating hard and fast with anticipation. With excitement. With wanting.

And then he tilted his head so he could press his lips to hers and Carly knew only in that first touch of his mouth how hungry she'd been for it. Starved, in fact.

This kiss was different than the two that had come before, though. Deeper. Richer. Like heavy cream compared to skim milk.

His lips were warm and wonderfully adept as they parted over hers, urged hers to part, too.

His other hand came to the side of her face, drawing her closer still, as his mouth opened farther, enticing hers to do the same as his tongue began to explore the sensitive inside of her lips, the tips of her teeth, her tongue...

This was a kiss that teased and courted and meant business at the same time, as mouths opened wide and tongues danced and parried so freely Carly wondered why they hadn't been doing this all along since they were so good at it.

And they *were* good at it. As good as if they'd been doing it forever.

He knew just when to be aggressive, just when to be subtle. When to be bold and in command. When to let her take the lead.

He knew how to light a fire in her blood so that flames ignited every secret spot in her body and made her ache to be touched, to feel his arms around her, his hands other places...

But before that happened, he stopped, ending the kiss with a determination that seemed reluctant, leaving Carly hungry for more.

He half sat, half fell back against the couch cushion the way he'd been before, looking at her again with eyes that seemed to regret the abrupt conclusion to what they'd been sharing so intently. So pleasantly...

"You're a dangerous woman, Carly Winters," he said in a raspy voice that partly teased and partly didn't.

"I've been told that," she said, seizing the teasing part to answer with a joke of her own.

She looked up into his eyes and knew what he was thinking as clearly as if the thoughts were in her own head. He was remembering two wives, one a mistake, and a daughter he was determined to protect from hurt.

And Carly understood why he hadn't wanted the kiss to go on, to go further.

Even though it left her yearning and burning inside.

But for her own sake, too, she knew it was best. It was one thing to practice getting to know someone new and another thing altogether to lose herself in the man the way she just had.

"I think it's time for me to call it a day," she said, swinging her legs to the floor. She slipped on her sandal, gathered up her discarded bandage and her crutches.

"You don't have to walk me to the cottage," she said in a hurry when Bax started to his feet to do just that. "Truly. It'll be better to clear my head if you don't."

Because she knew what would happen at the cottage door. He'd kiss her again. And once he did she wasn't sure either of them would stop it.

"Just stay where you are," she added more strongly than she felt.

And then she made her exit, wishing it could be more graceful.

Wishing more that she wasn't making it at all. That she was right back on that couch with him, his mouth locked onto hers, his hands in unspeakable places sharing the delight with the rest of her body.

And somehow Carly also knew as she went out into the breezeway alone that sleep wasn't going to come easily tonight. That her bed was going to seem awfully empty and lonely.

Because what she had no choice but to admit to herself was that she had a weak spot for Bax.

A very, very sweet weak spot...

Chapter Ten

Ordinarily Carly appreciated a little irony. But the irony of making up her mind to spend time with Bax and then not seeing him was hard to appreciate.

And by three o'clock Friday afternoon as she and her mother finished their visit to the town boarding-house, Carly had not laid eyes on Bax since leaving him sitting in the living room on Wednesday night after the hot kiss that had knocked her socks off.

The boardinghouse was actually Elk Creek's version of an old folks' home. It had been the original schoolhouse, and when the new one had been built, the Partridge sisters had bought the old building with the intention of turning it into a hotel. But there wasn't a lot of call for a hotel in the small town, and economics had required that Lurlene and Effie change course. So it had become the boardinghouse, and from there the boarders had proved to be mainly elderly people unable to live alone any longer.

Currently there were eight women and three men renting rooms from Lurlene and Effie, all of them considerably older than the fifty-nine-year-old twins and in various stages of needing assistance.

The beauty of the place was that everyone helped everyone else—the more capable picking up the slack for the less capable. And since no one was too infirm, it all worked out very well and left Lurlene and Effie free for other pursuits along with overseeing the house and providing meals.

Carly had been ending her Friday afternoons there for as long as she could remember. Sometimes she played cards with some of the residents, sometimes she read to them, sometimes she danced with old Mr. Elton who swore no one could cut a rug the way Carly could.

And always she brought what she was asked to bring—the newest movie released on video, library books, a bottle of brandy for Mrs. Gordon who insisted she was a teetotaler and couldn't possibly go into the liquor store to buy the brandy she needed purely for medicinal purposes.

Carly had said her goodbyes on the Friday before—certain it was her last—but since she was still in town this week, she didn't want to pass up the opportunity to see everyone one last time. Only today she'd asked her mother to come along, too, to drive her and help her carry in the shopping bag full of things one phone call had told her they all wanted.

Carly and her mother were just leaving the two-story Georgian redbrick when she heard, "Hey, stranger!"

She glanced up from watching the front stoop stairs as she descended them to find Bax and Evie Lee coming up the walk.

"Well, hello, Dr. McDermot," Carly's mother said before Carly could.

"Call me Bax, please, Mrs. Winters," he answered.

"And I'm Madge," Carly's mother responded.

Carly had already heard her mother's stamp of approval for the new doctor, and it was there again in the tone of her voice.

"Hi," Carly said somewhat belatedly.

It was funny, but just that initial sight of him was at once a balm and a tonic to her spirit. Not that she'd been aware of feeling in need of either, but one glance at him—even in cowboy boots, a pair of faded blue jeans and an old chambray shirt that made him look as if he'd just come from working the range—and it was as if everything inside her was set right again.

"Hi, Carly!" Evie Lee chimed in, helping Carly to broaden her spectrum.

"Hi, sweetie."

"We came to talk to a baby-sitter," Evie Lee announced.

"Carly knows, Evie. She recommended Miss Effie," Bax said to his daughter. Then to Carly he said,

"Where've you been? I haven't seen hide nor hair of you. And I've been lookin'," he added slightly under his breath and with a note of intimacy that erupted little tingles of delight in her bloodstream.

It also didn't hurt to know he'd missed her.

"I helped Deana with some paperwork for summer school yesterday and we went to the movies last night. This morning I was at my sister's house, and this afternoon—"

"She always visits here on Friday afternoons," Madge interjected, sounding proud but also a bit like Carly's sales representative.

Carly just wasn't sure what her mother was selling, though.

"Where have you been?" Carly countered, figuring if he could ask her point-blank, she could do the same with him.

"Spent yesterday mostly at the office, going over files and settlin' in—I sneaked in the back way so nobody'd know I was there. We had Ry's bachelor party last night so Evie Lee and I both slept over and today I helped get things ready for the wedding. Until a little while ago when Evie and I came in to keep our appointment with Miss Effie and get dressed for tonight."

That accounted for why their paths hadn't crossed although Carly wasn't too thrilled with the news that Bax had spent the previous evening at a bachelor party.

Not that it was any of her business.

"Are you ladies comin' to the wedding?" Bax

asked then, including Madge with the question even though his interest seemed more on Carly.

"I'm afraid I can't make it," Madge answered first again. "I have to stay with Hope and the children. I've already sent my regrets."

"Sorry to hear that. How 'bout you, Carly?"

"I'll be there." Eagerly since it meant seeing him, but she didn't add that.

"Goin' with anybody special?"

"Deana and her sister."

"How 'bout goin' with me...and Evie Lee instead?"

"Oh, that would be nice," Madge answered before Carly could. "Deana wouldn't mind. She has her sister to go with anyway."

Carly shot a curious glance at her mother, wondering what she was up to.

But whatever it was, Carly wasn't about to turn Bax down, if that was what her mother thought.

"What do you say?" Bax asked.

"Won't you be busy? I know you're one of the groomsmen and Evie Lee is the flower girl," Carly hedged just so she wouldn't appear to be too much of a pushover.

"That's only during the ceremony. We'll be free agents after that."

He said that with a smile that made it seem as if he and Carly were sharing a secret, and Carly couldn't have refused him even if she'd wanted to.

But once more her mother beat her to the punch. "Won't that be nice—to be together for the reception. Carly would be happy to go with you."

Carly gave her mother a sideways look, then glanced back at Bax to find him amused.

"What do you say?" he asked in a tone that focused on her alone.

"Okay. I suppose that would be all right."

"Great."

"And tomorrow night," Madge added then, "we're having a little dinner and ice cream and cake for Carly's birthday. Would you and Evie Lee like to come?"

Carly looked at her mother again, more directly this time, knowing for sure that Madge had something up her sleeve. Something that rang of matchmaking.

"Tomorrow's your birthday?" Bax asked Carly.

"Guess I can't deny it now."

"I'll go! I'll go!" Evie Lee answered eagerly.

"We like birthday parties," Bax said, including himself in his daughter's enthusiasm.

Madge took it as an acceptance of her invitation. "Oh, good. We're having it at Hope's house. You can just come with Carly."

"We'll be lookin' forward to it."

"So will we," Madge said, poking Carly with an elbow.

Bax looked at his watch. "We'd better get inside or Miss Effie will think we have bad manners."

Carly was only too happy to have this encounter end despite how good it was to see him. Her mother's antics were beginning to border on embarrassing.

"What time do you need to be out at the ranch tonight?" Carly asked then.

"We can leave about six-thirty."

His eyes were on hers again, giving off a warmth that seeped in through her pores and heated her all over.

"Six-thirty," she repeated. "I'll be ready."

"She'll be ready," her mother repeated as if Madge would personally make sure of it.

They all said goodbye then, and Bax and Evie Lee went inside as Carly and her mother made their way to Madge's car.

"What was that all about?" Carly demanded as they both got into the sedan.

"What was what about?" Madge said innocently.

"You know what. Accepting his offer for me to go to the wedding with him, inviting him for tomorrow night."

"I was just being friendly."

"You were being more than friendly. You were trying to set us up."

"Why would I do something like that when you're about to leave town?"

"Good question. You tell me."

"I wouldn't think of such a silly thing," Madge said. But then she added slyly, "Even though it's as plain as the nose on your face that he likes you and you like him."

Madge wasn't as straightforward as Deana, but Carly knew her mother was no happier about her plans to leave town than her friend was. And that, in her own way, Madge had the same hope that Bax could alter Carly's plans.

"I do like Bax," Carly admitted, realizing as she did just how true it was. "But that doesn't change anything. I'm still going to travel."

Madge didn't respond. She just poked her chin in the air and pretended to concentrate on her driving.

But even without any more comment from her mother, Carly had an inordinate urge to repeat herself, to impress upon her mother that she meant what she said, to put more force behind it.

She controlled the impulse, though, knowing too much protest would only prove her mother's point.

Carly hadn't cursed the crutches quite as much as she did that evening when she dressed for the wedding.

After a shower, a shampoo, air drying her hair to a silky sheen and carefully applying just enough makeup to accentuate her features, she slipped into a slinky black dress she'd bought with the idea of looking as sophisticated as she imagined everyone else would in cities like New York or London or Paris.

The dress was silk crepe with spaghetti straps, a hem at midthigh and a cut so perfect it skimmed her body just close enough to hint at what was beneath it without actually giving anything away.

She also had a pair of barely there three-inch heels and sheer black hose to go with it. But the whole effect was less than perfect with a bandage wrapped around her foot and ankle, and the wooden crutches as accessories.

And less than perfect was not what she was aiming for. She wanted to look absolutely perfect.

Not because she'd be seeing so many friends and family at the wedding. But because she'd be there with Bax.

She wished that wasn't the case, but what was the sense in kidding herself? She hadn't dug out the dress she considered her Paris dress to wow people who had known her since she was in diapers. It was Bax she wanted to wow.

It was Bax she was doing everything for lately.

Bax she really did like...

Admitting as much to her mother that afternoon in front of the boardinghouse kept niggling at her.

The moment she'd said it, she'd known that *liking* him was an understatement. A serious understatement.

But if she didn't just *like* him, then what did she feel about him?

"Don't think about it," she advised herself.

Because if she thought about it, she might have more to deal with than just being attracted to the man. And the attraction was enough to deal with all by itself. Add feelings to it that were more than mere *liking* him, and then where would she be?

Maybe not in Paris or London or Rome or New York.

"So just don't think about it!" she said more vehemently.

And for once she took her own advice.

Because it was one thing to come to terms with wanting to spend time with him while she was still in Elk Creek, but even thinking about feeling anything more serious about Bax was not something she could do. Not without risking things she wasn't willing to risk.

So instead, she told herself there wasn't anything to think about and she put on a mauve-colored lipstick, jammed the crutches under her arms and headed for the main house.

Before being alone led to anymore delving into things she didn't want to delve into.

Attraction. Infatuation. That was all that was going on with her when it came to Bax, she swore to herself as she crossed the breezeway.

Simple attraction and infatuation that came out of enjoying his company, out of having fun with him, out of not being blind to his charms, his handsomeness, his sexiness.

But it was nothing as serious as what had gone on between her and Jeremy.

Nothing as life-altering as that.

So she was still safe.

"You're here!" Evie Lee said when Carly knocked on the back door a few minutes later. "Could you do my hair so it looks nice? Daddy says he's just gonna put a brush in it and leave it and that won't be pretty enough for a flower girl."

"How about a braid like we did that first time?" Carly suggested, grateful for the distraction of the little girl in the frilly midnight-blue dress with the silver sash.

After all, who could think about silly things like feelings when Evie Lee had a hair crisis?

"Evie Lee? Where are you? I need to brush your hair now or we'll be late."

Bax's voice came from upstairs and just that was enough to make everything inside Carly stand up and take notice.

"Carly's here and she's gonna do my hair," Evie Lee hollered back.

"Thank heaven for small favors," he called in return.

Evie Lee went running out of the kitchen then, returning moments later with a hairbrush and a rubber band.

Carly had pulled a chair away from the table and sat in it so Evie Lee could stand in front of her. Which Evie Lee did, with a twirling flourish to make her skirt billow out around her.

"Did you get to meet Miss Effie?" Carly asked as she French-braided the little girl's hair.

"Uh-huh."

"Did you like her?"

"She's nice. Like a gramma. She's gonna baby-sit me when my daddy goes to work and she said we could bake cookies and go to the park and stuff."

"That sounds good." And more appealing than Carly wanted to admit. Appealing enough to cause Carly a twinge of jealousy to add to the list of feelings she didn't want to explore.

"But she doesn't know 'bout makin' French braids and puttin' pencils in my hair. That's one bad thing," Evie Lee was saying. "I won't be pretty if you go away."

The little girl's words didn't come out plaintively, but the statement made Carly's heart ache anyway as she recalled what Bax had said about all his daughter had been through with her stepmother and the blow her self-esteem had taken.

"You're pretty no matter what anyone does with your hair," she told the child.

"But I'm prett*er* when you do it nice."

"How about if I talk to Deana about doing your hair for you sometimes, on special occasions? She's just next door and I'll bet she'd be happy to," Carly suggested, wondering as she did why the thought of Deana taking her place didn't sit any better than the idea of Evie Lee baking cookies and going to the park with Effie Partridge rather than with her. Especially when it wasn't really *her* place at all to do any of those things with Bax's daughter.

"Okay," Evie Lee agreed reluctantly. "But it won't be the same as when you do it."

"It won't be the same for me, either," Carly heard herself say in a quiet voice that surprised her.

"What won't be the same?" Bax asked as he came into the kitchen.

Carly didn't glance up from what she was doing, but just the sound of his voice closer by, the feel of his presence in the room, erupted a whole new set of feelings too powerful to ignore.

"It won't be the same if the lady next door combs

my hair into a braid the way Carly does when Carly goes away.''

"Are you leavin' sooner than I thought?'' Bax asked with what could have been a note of alarm in his tone, although Carly wasn't sure.

"Not until my ankle heals,'' she answered.

"So you're just making provisions for the future.''

Provisions that rubbed her wrong.

"We were just talking,'' she said, finishing Evie Lee's braid to look up at Bax for the first time since he'd joined them.

There weren't a lot of men in Elk Creek who could wear a tuxedo and seem as right in it as they did in blue jeans. But Bax was one of them. And a single glance at him was enough to take Carly's breath away.

Tall, lean, muscular, and very dashing—he still bore a hint of rugged masculinity.

He didn't have the entire tux on, though. The jacket was in place—hanging from broad shoulders as if it had been cut especially to accommodate them—and he wore the flawlessly tailored pants, the crisp white shirt and the bow tie. But he was carrying the cummerbund in one hand.

He held it up and said, "Would you consider doing me next?''

Again Carly couldn't be sure if his voice was flecked with something more than his words conveyed. But the half smile and the quirk to his eyebrow lent credence to what she took as innuendo.

And there were a number of things she could

think of to do with him, none of them as innocent as helping him on with his cummerbund.

"I wanna see me!" Evie Lee announced then, dashing out of the kitchen to leave Carly alone with Bax in a stew of sexually charged air.

"I can't hook this thing to save my life," he said then, referring once more to the waistband. "Would you mind?"

"No," she answered simply, succinctly, unable to say more because her head was still swimming with other thoughts about him and the effect that the sight of him was having on her, making her pulse race and little sparks dance in the pit of her stomach.

Bax slipped off the suit coat and draped it over one of the chairs. Then he came to stand where Evie Lee had been moments before, turning his back to Carly.

It didn't help matters that she was eye level with his rear end. Or that the trousers smoothed across it just so, leaving no doubt that it was a great male derriere.

"I don't even know which way is up and which is down with this thing," he was saying, but to Carly the words seemed to come from a long way away as she fought an inordinate urge to see that terrifically sexy posterior bare of everything.

Then she caught herself and realized she needed to say something in response.

"Here, let me see it," she finally managed to reply.

She assumed from the shape of the cummerbund that the straight edge was the bottom and the arched edge the top. But having decided that, she was left in need of reaching around Bax to set it at his waist.

Not a good idea.

Because once her arms were around his middle, that was just where they wanted to stay. Her arms around him, her cheek pressed to his hard back...

But of course she couldn't do that and she told herself in no uncertain terms to stop these unwelcome thoughts and behave herself.

Although it was difficult to heed her own warnings when his hands brushed hers as he tried to hold the front of the cummerbund in place to free her to fasten the back. That simple contact sent shards of glittering delight straight into her bloodstream. Not only did she want to keep her arms around him, to press her cheek to his back, but she wanted to feel more of his touch against her hands, sliding up her arms, pressing her to him...

The yearning for all that got so strong, Carly could hear the blood rushing through her veins and she knew if she didn't pull herself together in a hurry she'd be sunk. So she reclaimed her hands, made quick work of hooking the waistband, and said, "There!" much too cheerily.

"Thanks," he said, his own voice an octave lower than usual for no reason Carly could fathom.

Then he stepped away, retrieved his jacket from the chair back and put it on.

"Yep, feels like a monkey suit, all right," he said as he tugged at his cuffs and set everything right.

"You look wonderful," Carly heard herself say softly and much too breathlessly before she even knew she was going to voice what was going through her mind.

Bax only acknowledged the compliment with a rakish smile before motioning to her with one hand as if he were trying to levitate her. "Come on, let me get a gander at you."

Ogling him was one thing. Carly was less comfortable being the ogle-ee.

But she could hardly stay sitting there, so she used the table for support and stood without the crutches to mar the effect.

His sea-foam-green eyes went from her head to her toes and back up again—the return trip accompanied by a long, slow whistle of approval.

"Now there's a good example of a little bit of a dress leavin' just enough to the imagination to whet a man's appetite," he said appreciatively, clearly enjoying the sight for a moment longer before tossing another glance downward. "But what about that high heel?"

"What about it?" Carly asked with a look down at her only shod foot.

"High heels and crutches don't mix."

"I did just fine coming over here."

"You're riskin' broken bones," he warned.

"I'll be okay."

"Either that or you'll end up with worse than a sprained ankle. But then, on second thought, that'd keep you around longer, so I guess I should just shut my mouth."

Evie Lee rejoined them then, saying as she did, "Isn't it time to go?"

Bax seemed reluctant to take his eyes off Carly, but with his daughter insinuating herself between them he didn't have much choice.

"Daddy? Did you hear me? Isn't it time to go?" the little girl repeated when she didn't get an instant response.

"I suppose it is," he said, still without taking his eyes off Carly, all the while smiling that secret smile that somehow seemed to wrap the two of them in their own private cocoon.

"Then let's go," Evie Lee persisted.

Bax took a deep breath and sighed it out as if he would have preferred staying there indefinitely, giving Carly the once-over.

But then he reached for her crutches, keeping them away from her. "You're sure about this?" he asked.

"I'm an expert on those things by now," she assured him.

He gave her a dubious, sideways glance, but handed them over and Carly got up onto them with aplomb. Then she headed across the kitchen to prove her ability.

"What did I tell you?" she said as she made it to the swinging door.

But when she glanced over her shoulder to see if he was admiring her competency, she instead discovered him admiring something else—her derriere—before he realized he'd been caught at it. He simply raised his gaze and smiled a wicked smile.

"Oh yeah, you're good," he said, this time with too much innuendo to mistake.

He stepped up to push the swinging door open for her and once she and Evie Lee had gone through it and were headed for the front door, Bax made his way to Carly's side to keep a hand at the small of her back just in case she stumbled.

And as far as Carly was concerned, that was only a benefit of the high heels and crutches combination.

A benefit that was worth whatever risk she was taking.

Chapter Eleven

The wedding was held outside on the patio at the McDermot ranch. White lanterns were strung all around, their strings wrapped in vines and white roses. The aisle down which Tallie Shanahan walked was bordered with candles on white pillars that were also wrapped in vines and roses, and she came to a stop in front of the minister where she and Ry met beneath an archway trimmed to match.

It was a beautiful ceremony, with Ry's brothers standing as groomsmen, his sister, Kate, and Tallie's friends, Maya and Kansas, serving as the brides-maids.

Since this was the first Elk Creek had seen of the fourth McDermot brother, Matt, and the sole sister, Kate, they drew almost as much attention and curi-

ous stares as the bride and groom. But from where
Carly sat with Deana and Deana's sister in the rows
of white chairs set out for the guests, she only had
eyes for Bax.

All the brothers were strikingly handsome men.
But to Carly, only Bax stood out from the crowd
and she could hardly wait for the I dos to be said
and the kiss to be over so she could have him by
her side again.

But before that could happen, Tallie and Ry were
presented as man and wife. While all the guests filed
through a receiving line to congratulate the happy
couple, tables were set up and the rows of chairs
were dispersed around them.

Out came a fully stocked bar and by the time
everyone was ready to sit down, an elaborate dinner
of poached salmon, crown rib roast, new potatoes,
grilled vegetables, Caesar salad, French bread and
wine was served.

Evie Lee had met up with other kids and was
more interested in playing than in eating, and since
Deana and Deana's sister shared a table with Bax
and Carly, conversation was general but lively.

Only after the meal, when the band began to play
dance music, were Carly and Bax left alone as Deana and her sister were led onto the floor by some
of the single men.

"Don't let me keep you if you're dying to trip
the light fantastic," Carly felt obliged to say.

"I think I can live one night without dancing,"
Bax said wryly.

It was a relief to Carly. She would have been

crushed if he'd gone off to dance with some of the other single women who kept throwing him come-hither smiles.

"What about you?" he asked. "I met a man at the boardinghouse today who told me to get that ankle of yours fixed up on the double so you could get to dancin' with him again."

"Mr. Elton," Carly said. "I think he keeps forgetting that I'm leaving town and won't be there to dance with him one way or another."

"He also said if he was a little younger, he'd be waltzing you down the aisle."

Carly laughed. "He's a character."

"*Has* anybody ever waltzed you down the aisle?"

"You mean, have I ever been married? Somewhere in my deep, dark, mysterious past?"

"Something like that."

"Nope. Never."

"Are the men around here crazy or blind or what?"

"I think they must be," she deadpanned. "It isn't as if I haven't had the chance, though. I was engaged, as a matter of fact, until about five months ago."

"You were?"

"To a man named Jeremy Smythe. He worked for the newspaper that serves all four counties. But he lived in Elk Creek. At least, he did before we broke up. Then he moved to Pinewood."

"I drove through Pinewood on my way here. It's a lot like Elk Creek."

"Small town in the center of farms and ranches—

it's a *lot* like Elk Creek. It would have to be to get Jeremy to move there.'' She hadn't meant that to sound as disparaging as it had.

''Who broke up with whom?''

''I guess I did it. But not without provocation.''

''He was a cheater? A con artist? A manipulative creep?'' Bax guessed with levity and a splash of hopefulness in his tone.

''He misled me.''

''Ah, a liar.''

Carly flinched. ''Jeremy isn't a bad guy. It's just...well, like I said, he misled me.''

''How?''

Carly glanced out at the wedding celebration they were in the midst of, realizing as she did that Bax had a way of focusing so intently on her that it was almost as if they were alone. It helped her confide in him even though she hesitated.

''I've always wanted to travel. I told you that.''

''About getting the bug from your aunt when you were a kid,'' he said, proving he really did listen to what she told him.

''Right. I've been to Cheyenne and Denver, to Las Vegas on a junket some teachers took, but that's it. I've never seen an ocean. I've never been to Disneyland. I want to go to the Smithsonian. I want to see the White House and the Eiffel Tower. I want to see the leaves change color in Vermont in the autumn. I want to spend Christmas in London, New Year's Eve in New York. I want to see Paris. I want to see Spain and Greece and Ireland and Scotland

and all of Europe. I want to see China and Japan. I want to ride the Orient Express and—''

She cut herself off, knowing she'd gotten carried away on her favorite topic.

''Anyhow,'' she said with a laugh as she got back to the point. ''From the time we met two years ago, all through our year-long engagement, Jeremy made me think he wanted to do it all, too. With me. That we were going to travel the world together.''

''But it never happened.''

''No, it never happened. I'd talk and talk, and he'd say he wanted to go, too. But not only didn't he ever take any steps to make it happen, when *I* would, he'd throw a wrench into the works. He'd all of a sudden have some kind of health problem. He'd have back spasms, he'd think he might be on the verge of gallbladder surgery—which he never had. Once he thought maybe he had kidney stones— something else he never had. Or he'd swear his folks needed him home. And every time, he'd tell me I was just selfish to be thinking about traveling when there were other things more important. Then, of course, I'd cancel the trip.''

''Until…'' Bax prompted.

''Until he told me he couldn't get away from work and I found out otherwise.''

''How did you do that?''

''I found out it wasn't that he *couldn't* get away. The truth was that he *wouldn't* get away. I had his editor's daughter in a class and during a conference the man started to tell me how thrilled the paper would be if we ever got our act together and started that traveling we were always talking about. Apparently the newspaper had offered to continue Jeremy's salary if he kept writing articles and columns about our travel experiences and faxed them in. Jeremy had told me two days before that he couldn't leave because the paper had refused to let him do just that.''

"So he was a liar."

That still sounded so harsh. But it was true. Carly just didn't confirm it outright.

"I confronted him, and along with telling me more about how selfish I was, how I only thought of myself, he finally admitted that he didn't want the same things I did. He'd only acted like he did to hook me. But when it came right down to it, he didn't want to travel—he didn't *like* to travel—and he was actually intimidated by the thought of going outside the confines of small-town living. In fact, he'd figured if he could just get me to the altar, I'd forget all about the rest of the world, settle down and quit dreaming my silly dreams—that was how he put it. He said if we just got married and had a few babies, I'd get to like the life I'd been born to— again, those were his words.''

"Sounds like it was a good thing you found out what was on his mind before you married him."

"That's what I thought." Although it had still been difficult. And painful. She'd cared about Jeremy. She'd thought they were going to see the world together. She'd looked forward to it.

"So you broke it off with him," Bax said, coming full circle.

"So I broke it off with him." And in the process felt disillusioned and disappointed and angry with herself for letting him manipulate her as long as he had. Angry with herself for letting her feelings for Jeremy blind her to what was really going on, to the fact that he was doing his best to pen her in. Angry with herself for wondering if her dreams really were silly...

"And then you packed your bags," Bax said, interrupting her thoughts.

"First, I agreed to finish out the school year, applied for a sabbatical from my teaching job and put my house up for rent."

"And *then* you packed your bags."

"And sprained my ankle." And met you...

"And now, as soon as you're back on two feet, you're going to see all those places by yourself."

He'd said that in an upbeat way. So why had it sounded so lonely to her?

She ignored the feeling. "Just as soon as I can."

Bax leaned in close and said, "For what it's worth, I don't think your dreams are silly. The world is an amazing place, and there's nothing wrong with wanting to see it."

The man truly had a knack for saying the right thing.

"Thank you for that," she said quietly. "And you've seen some of it, so you're talking from experience, right?"

"Right. I haven't done the Orient or been everywhere you mentioned in the States, but I've been enough places to know there are things out there worth seein'. And as for the guy thinking you'd just forget about what you want if he could tie you down—big mistake. Nobody wants to be *tied down*."

"That's what your ex-wife said, isn't it? About Evie Lee."

He confirmed that with raised eyebrows. "It's good that you know what you want and are going after it straightforwardly, without hurting anybody else in the process. There's nothing wrong with wanting to get out a little, see some things. For me, doing that and living in some big cities along the way helped me know better when I was ready to make the commitment to a family. It made me appreciate places like Elk Creek all the more. That other guy was dead wrong thinking to steal that from you and expectin' that you'd be content without it."

Again, all the right things to say.

But somehow Carly thought Bax looked and sounded a little sad saying them.

Then he sat up tall in his chair, as if someone had infused him with energy and put a devilish smile on his face. "For now, though, I have you where I want you and I think we could use some champagne. What do you say I snitch us a bottle? If I'm not mistaken, it's French, so we can consider it warming you up for your trip to Paris."

"Sounds good."

"I'll be right back."

He left then, in search of the champagne, and Carly watched him work his way through the guests—some he knew and some who introduced themselves along the way. And as she kept her eye on him, she couldn't help wondering what was really going through his mind, if her talking about being penned in had brought up too many memories of his ex-wife, or if he was sorry to hear the same sentiment from her.

But by the time he got back he seemed in such high spirits that she forgot to think any more about it.

Instead, she let herself be carried away by his charm, his wit, all the attention he lavished on her, and those good looks that were enough to wipe out every other thought she'd ever had.

She let herself just revel in being with him.

Because if she couldn't be in New York or London or Paris, there wasn't another place on the planet she'd rather have been than with Bax.

Carly and Bax didn't leave the wedding reception until nearly eleven and the party was still going strong. For everyone but Evie Lee. She was exhausted to the point of being slaphappy so they said their good-nights and went home.

Because it was so late and Bax had to help his daughter out of her flower girl dress, Carly left him to it and made her own way to the cottage, wishing the night wasn't over, but resigning herself to the fact that it was.

The problem, though, was that after hours in the summer night air, the cottage felt hot and stuffy. And since she wasn't actually tired, she opted for a quick change of clothes—cutoff shorts and a simple tank top—opened all the windows to let in some of the cooler air, and went outside to sit on the swing that had hung between the two huge elm trees in the backyard for as long as she could remember.

She sat on the single plank seat, dropped her crutches to the ground and hooked her elbows around the ropes that connected it to the tree branches, but she didn't put the swing into motion. She just rested there, letting her head fall to one of the ropes as her gaze wandered up to the main house.

The house where Bax was at that very moment.

The kitchen light was on downstairs, but so was the hall light upstairs and his bedroom light, too. The curtain wasn't drawn on his bedroom window and even though she saw him pass by the window several times—wearing less of the tux with each passing—it wasn't as if he were standing right there and she could watch him undress.

But she was imagining it just the same. Remembering what he had looked like that first day when she'd caught him coming out of the shower wearing only jeans. And what he'd looked like that evening at the ranch when he'd shed his shirt after riding that wild stallion.

She was remembering, too, what had gone through her when she'd fastened his cummerbund earlier. Remembering watching him during the wedding ceremony. And all through the evening.

And she thought that it was the hardest thing she'd ever done not to get off that swing and go into the house, up the stairs to that bedroom, to do more than just watch.

He came to the window then. To open it more than it was.

Carly was sitting perfectly still, so she didn't know what caught his attention, but something did because she saw him take a second look to see what—or who—was out there.

When he recognized her, he waved. Smiled. Then disappeared.

The light went out in the bedroom and Carly assumed he'd gone to bed, leaving her to fight images of that on top of everything else.

But then she saw a shadow move in front of the kitchen window and there he was again, this time coming out the back door to be with her after all.

He'd put on a plain white T-shirt and a pair of disreputable jeans with a rip at the knee. He was barefoot—just as she was—and he looked so incredible that her mouth nearly watered at the sight. Certainly her pulse picked up speed.

"What are you doin' out here?" he asked as he crossed the yard to her.

"I guess I didn't get enough fresh air tonight." Or enough of him, either, but she didn't add that.

"Want a push?" he offered, nodding at the swing.

"No, that's okay. It makes more noise than you'd think."

He went around behind her then, to the park bench that nestled between the two tree trunks under the canopy of the elms' entwined branches where her mother had spent summer afternoons reading in the shade. He sat with one foot on the seat so his knee could brace an elbow and made himself comfortable.

Carly spun around to face him, letting the ropes cross over her head. "Aren't you tired?" she asked.

"Nope, can't say I am," he said with a glance that seemed to take her in all at once and let her know she was the cause of his insomnia. Just as he was the cause of hers.

"What's up for tomorrow?" she asked, just to make conversation.

"I'm part of the cleanup crew out at the ranch. That'll probably take most of the day. Then we have your birthday party tomorrow night, as I recall. Happy birthday—almost—by the way."

"Thanks. But you don't have to go to the party if you don't want to. I know my mother sort of put you on the spot."

"I wouldn't miss it," he said emphatically.

"I have to warn you that my two aunts are slightly eccentric. They'll both get crushes on you the minute you walk in the door. They do it with any man who pays them a visit—that's how they'll see you being there, paying *them* a visit."

"Are you telling me that it doesn't have anything to do with me personally?"

"Don't take offense," Carly confirmed with a laugh. "I'm just letting you know that my aunt Gloria will follow you like a puppy while Aunt Tasha will flirt outrageously the whole night—even if both of them have trouble recalling your name."

"I see. Well, I think I can handle it. I know all

too well what it's like to have a crush,'' he said pointedly, his eyes shooting a message all their own that seemed to warm the cool night air around them.

Then he poked his chin her way. ''Why don't you come over here and let me rub your foot?''

There were things she wanted him to rub, but tonight her foot wasn't one of them.

''It's late and we'd have to unwrap it and I'd have to wrap it all over again. It's okay.''

''Then why don't you just come over here and sit with me?''

Said the spider to the fly...

But it was an invitation Carly couldn't resist. An invitation she didn't want to resist.

So she didn't.

When he reached out a hand to her, she took it and let him pull her gently to sit beside him on the bench.

Then he stretched his arm along the seat back behind her but not touching her. Much as she wished he would because she craved the feel of his arm around her.

''So, is this crush you mentioned recent?'' she heard herself ask, flirting more than she knew she should.

''Mmm. As we speak,'' he answered with a hint of that secret smile toying with his lips.

''Anybody I know?'' she persisted, aware that she was playing with fire. And not caring.

''I think you've met once or twice. She's a little bit of a woman with brown hair that shines red in the sun, eyes the color of topaz, and skin like cream. I think she used to teach junior high geography.''

''Doesn't sound like anybody I know,'' Carly joked even as she flushed beneath his compliment and the scrutiny that went with it.

''The trouble is,'' he continued, pretending he was greatly wounded, ''she doesn't know I'm alive.''

''I can't believe that,'' Carly countered as if they weren't talking about her. ''I'll bet she notices more about you than you think.''

That seemed to please him. ''I wonder,'' he said hopefully.

He was looking into her eyes, giving her more of the secret smile as he seemed to search for something.

She didn't know what. But she did know that sitting there the way they were, surrounded by the darkness of night, shadowed even from the moon by the tree branches, she felt removed from everything but Bax.

Every sense was tuned in to him. Every nerve ending cried out for his touch. And nothing else seemed to matter but that moment. The two of them. The charge of pure sexual energy in the air around them...

Bax cupped her chin in the circle of his thumb and forefinger then and tilted her face up a little more so his mouth could find hers, slowly, softly, warmly.

Carly's eyes drifted closed as she gave herself

over to his kiss, a kiss she'd been craving since the last one they'd shared the night before.

His arm came around her from the back of the bench, his other slipped under her knees and he lifted her to his lap so he could hold her closer and deepen the kiss even as his lips parted farther and his tongue came to play.

Maybe it was all the champagne she'd had at the wedding reception. Maybe it was the intoxication of the night air. Or the intoxication of just being in his arms, but Carly felt no doubts, no reticence, no hesitation.

She was where she wanted to be. With this man who seemed to have gotten into her bloodstream, into her every waking thought and a fair share of her dreams, into her heart...

He kissed her with a new intensity. A new hunger, as if what they'd shared before had only whetted his appetite.

And Carly answered every bit of it with an intensity, a hunger of her own. She wrapped her arms around him, let her palms ride the hard muscles of his back, let them even slide beneath his shirt to indulge in the pure delight of the hard, bare expanse all the way to his broad shoulders.

His skin was smooth and warm and seemed to feed her soul, it felt so wonderful. Their kiss turned urgent and she could feel how much he wanted her as the sure sign of it rose against her hip. And she wanted him just as much. So much that it was an ache deep inside her. So much she couldn't help arching her back to let him know she needed more of his touch.

He was a quick study, slipping big, capable hands under her tank top to her bare back and then around just to her rib cage.

She didn't know if he was teasing her again or just taking his time, but she thought that if he didn't do more than that—and fast—she was going to shatter like blown glass under too great a pressure.

And then one hand started a languorous path upward until he found her breast, encasing it, kneading it, learning every curve.

Her breast had never been as sensitive as it was at that moment. Alive with wanting him and he made it come alive even more.

He found the hardened crest, circling it, pinching gently, rolling it and tugging at it and driving her wild.

She didn't know what there was between herself and Bax, what drew her so inescapably to him, but she knew there was magic to it. Magic to his touch. Magic to him and how much he could make her want him even without trying, let alone now, when her every sense was singing beneath his attentions.

She wanted him so much it hurt. Wanted him to go on kissing her forever. Touching her forever. She wanted to stay right there in his arms forever.

But for some reason that thought suddenly set off an alarm in her head.

Or maybe it was that thought along with having talked about Jeremy earlier so that, too, was fresh in her mind.

But whatever had set off the alarm, she couldn't stop thinking that it was feelings like she was having at that moment—feelings that had been less powerful for Jeremy than they already were for Bax—that had kept her from doing what she'd wanted. Feelings that had tied her to Elk Creek...

"No...no...we..."

It was difficult to get the words out. To give voice to the battle that was raging inside her between wanting Bax, wanting all he was doing to her, wanting what could come, and being terrified of what it might mean later on.

But he got the message.

His glorious hand retraced the path to her back and then he removed it from under her tank top.

His kiss softened, slowed. Stopped.

He laid his forehead against the top of her head and took several deep breaths.

"No?" he repeated.

"I just... Maybe this isn't a good idea," she finally managed to murmur.

He didn't say anything for a moment. He just let silence linger as he seemed to fight for some control of his own.

Then he said, "Okay. You're probably right."

He didn't sound totally convinced.

But then neither was she.

How could anything that felt as incomplete as this did be where they should stop?

But she knew it wouldn't be wise to start it up again, either, so she just let it alone and pushed herself off his lap to sit more primly beside him before her own willpower could get any weaker than it already was.

"I should...go in," she said, still stammering over words she didn't want to say because they distanced her further from what she really wanted. What her body was crying out for yet.

Bax nodded his agreement, but he didn't move. He looked almost as if he couldn't. As if he were incapable of it.

"I'm just gonna sit here a minute. Get myself...in order."

Ah. She hadn't thought about the advantage of a woman's body carrying all that desire on the inside rather than the outside the way a man's did.

"I'll see you tomorrow," he said then, as if he preferred being left alone.

"Okay."

Carly got up onto her crutches again and headed for the cottage without looking back because she was too afraid if she did she wouldn't be able to make herself go.

But his passion-husky voice stopped her halfway.

"Carly?"

"Yes?"

Silence again.

Carly waited.

But in the end all he said was, "Good night."

"Good night," she answered, knowing that wasn't all he'd intended to say without knowing what he had.

But there was so much on her own mind that she didn't try to explore his.

Instead, she went the rest of the way to the cottage, wondering how she was ever going to get any sleep when what she was taking to bed with her were raging, unsatisfied desires that no amount of reason could chase away.

And it occurred to her that she'd never in her life been so torn.

Because she wanted to leave Elk Creek to see the world as much as she always had.

Which was just about as much as she wanted Bax…

Chapter Twelve

The postwedding cleanup the next day took until the middle of the afternoon. By the time the job was finished Evie Lee had campaigned to spend the night at the ranch so Bax returned to Elk Creek alone.

He didn't go directly home, though. With Carly's birthday in mind he drove farther into town, down Center Street where the shops and businesses lined either side of the wide avenue in a long, facing row of quaint old buildings.

The particular shop he was looking for was about three quarters of the way to the train station that ended Center Street on the south. When he reached that particular shop, he parked nose-first in front of it.

The building was a single-story square box

painted white and trimmed with bright-blue awnings over the door and windows to break up the starkness. Inside was the local travel agency and a small luggage store combined.

Who could be easier to find a gift for than someone about to embark on a long trip? he thought. Travel alarm. Travel umbrella. Travel tote. There were any number of things he could get Carly for her birthday.

Except that as he sat in his car, staring at the place, Bax couldn't make himself get out and go in.

The problem with all those travel gift ideas was that they shouted encouragement for her to travel.

And how could he encourage what he found himself wishing like crazy wasn't in the offing?

That wasn't a good sign, he realized.

But there it was, washing through him like a tidal wave. He wanted her to leave about as much as he wanted to have open-heart surgery.

And for some reason, the force of just how much he didn't want her to leave surprised him.

What was all that stuff he'd thought before? About it being okay to have a brief encounter with someone he knew was leaving because knowing she was leaving would act like armor that would keep him from getting too close to her? From getting attached to her?

Well, so much for that.

That armor had apparently been as flimsy as tissue paper.

Because there he was, feeling both close to her and attached.

And hating the thought of her leaving so much that if it had been a wall, he'd have put his fist through it.

How had this happened? he asked himself as he stayed sitting in his car, staring at the travel agency as if it were evil incarnate.

But there was no clear answer because even though it hadn't taken much time, it still seemed to have sneaked up on him.

Maybe if he hadn't watched the way she was with the folks of Elk Creek—laughing and joking and listening delightedly to every story anyone wanted to tell her—maybe then he might not have developed a soft spot for her.

Maybe if he hadn't watched her with Evie Lee, giving his daughter the attention and bolstering that had made the little girl beam, maybe then he might not have come to appreciate Carly and every nuance about her.

Maybe if he hadn't heard what the elderly residents of the boardinghouse had had to say about her—how much she did for them, going out of her way to provide some of that same sort of attention she'd given Evie Lee and adding a little spice to their lives—maybe then he might not have started to just plain like her more than anyone he'd met in a long, long time.

Maybe if he hadn't studied the way her eyes glittered gold. Maybe if he hadn't noticed how shiny her hair was. How flawless her skin. How great her body. Maybe then he might not have found himself itching to touch her, to hold her, to make love to her.

Maybe if he hadn't done all those things, he wouldn't feel as if he had a lump of lead in his gut every time he thought of her leaving.

But he had done all those things.

And when they were added to that initial attraction that had nearly knocked him for a loop the first time he'd set eyes on her, it made for some damn overwhelming feelings rolling around inside him.

Feelings he hadn't bargained for when he'd decided to indulge in this time with her before she left.

Feelings that wouldn't let him get out of his car to buy her a gift that would say, *So long, have a nice trip....*

So he started the car engine again and backed away from the curb, parking a second time at the very end of Center Street in front of a store of an entirely different sort.

This tiny shop took up one storefront of a building that looked as if it had originally been a two-story Victorian house. Now it was split into three sections on the ground floor—the jewelry store, the barber shop and an accountant's office—with the local real estate office occupying the top floor.

But it wasn't a haircut, a tax return or a real estate investment he was interested in.

When he finally got out of the car, it was the jewelry store he headed for.

As he did, a small voice in the back of his head asked if jewelry might be too personal a gift.

But how could it be any more personal than the

way he felt about Carly? was the answer he gave himself. Because like it or not, what he was feeling about her was definitely personal.

The jeweler greeted him when he crossed the store's threshold. He was an older, bald-headed man who came out from behind a table where a bright work lamp lit pieces of a watch he was working on.

"What can we do for you today?" the shopkeeper asked.

Bax looked around, having no idea what he might actually buy.

His gaze settled on the first of three cases, but displayed there were engagement and wedding rings. And even though his glance hesitated there longer than it should have, he bypassed it. The second case held watches and cocktail rings, which seemed too *im*personal to him, but the third contained necklaces, bracelets and brooches and those seemed to strike a chord.

"I need a birthday gift," he informed the jeweler then, leaning over the case to have a look at what was inside.

Bax didn't have any trouble choosing. The first thing that caught his eye was a white-gold lariat necklace that he could just picture around the porcelain column of Carly's neck, dropping slightly below the hollow of her throat, the dangling ends pointing downward to those small breasts that tempted him beyond rational thought.

Those small breasts that had felt so incredible in his hand the night before....

He cleared his throat. "Let's have a look at that necklace," he said, pointing to the lariat.

The older man slipped it out of the case and onto a piece of black velvet to show it off to best effect.

"How much?"

The jeweler told him, but Bax barely heard the answer because he was still too lost in the mental image of how it would look on Carly. Instead, he merely said he'd take it, and waited while the shopkeeper wrapped it up for him.

It only struck him then that there might be more to the lariat's appeal than his simply liking it. What was he trying to do? Lasso her with it? that voice in his head asked again.

The idea didn't sit well with him. It wasn't something he wanted to do to her. And even if that was what he subconsciously had up his sleeve, he knew it was a futile attempt.

She's leaving one way or another, he told himself sternly. And again the truth of it was like sandpaper along an open wound.

Why was this bothering him so much all of a sudden? he wondered.

But he still couldn't figure it out.

"Is this for your wife?" the jeweler asked from where he was tying a red ribbon around the package.

"No. I'm not married," Bax answered.

"Must be for someone special, though," the man insisted. "Someone you care about."

"Mmm," was all Bax answered.

But he couldn't stop thinking about the man's

comment even as he paid for the necklace and took the small gift out to his car.

Someone he cared about...

Was that why the thought of Carly leaving was eating at him so persistently now? Because he *cared* about her?

Bax shied away from that notion as he backed out of the parking space and retraced his path up Center Street.

But even as he tried to think of other things, the idea that he'd come to care for Carly kept niggling at him.

Cared about...

What exactly did that mean? Besides that he didn't want her to leave town.

It was a troubling thought.

Because what occurred to him as he worried about it was that somehow, when he wasn't looking, when he'd least expected it, he'd gone right ahead and gotten in over his head with her.

In over his head with someone who was going to take off like a shot the minute she was able to and leave everything and everybody behind.

Was that something she realized? he wondered. That when she left this place she'd be leaving behind all the perks of this small town she seemed to fit so perfectly into? That she'd be leaving behind family and friends who loved her? Family and friends she seemed to revel in herself?

Surely she must have considered that.

But what if she hadn't? What if, in her determination to hightail it out of there, she'd overlooked much of what was great about Elk Creek and every-body in it?

Maybe someone could point it all out to her...

Okay, so it wasn't likely to make any difference, he admitted before his hopes could get too high.

But then again, pointing out to her what she'd be leaving behind couldn't do any harm, either.

Could it?

He didn't see how.

And if he didn't see how it could do any harm, then maybe he could put a little effort into it himself.

Because the more he thought about the fact that he cared about her, the more certain he was about one other thing.

There was a better than even chance that when she left, she'd take his heart along with her.

And that wasn't going to be any easier to lose than she was.

Because maybe...just maybe...he more than cared about her....

Carly's party that evening was at Hope's house around the block. Bax drove, but the ride was so short Carly didn't have time to do more than ask where Evie Lee was and hear the explanation before they were pulling up at the curb in front of her sister's place.

The house was much like Carly's—a two-story clapboard farmhouse—only it was painted Salem blue, trimmed in white and wore a Happy Birthday, Carly! banner strung from the porch eaves.

"Don't forget I warned you," Carly said to Bax as he turned off the engine.

He just smiled, got out of the car and rounded it to open her door.

He looked as handsome as ever, dressed in dark-blue jeans and a crisp white Western shirt with a collar and pointed yoke of midnight-blue, and as Carly eased out of the passenger side and onto her crutches she feasted on the sight out of the corner of her eye and wished she was spending the next few hours alone with him.

That wish wasn't granted for longer than it took them to reach the front porch before Carly's nephews burst from the house shouting jubilant happy birthdays to her.

And so the party began.

Bax was more the center of attention than Carly was, but she didn't mind. It gave her the chance to watch him from a distance. To study him. To enjoy the sight of the big man roughhousing with the little boys, exchanging sports anecdotes with her brother-in-law, good-naturedly humoring her mother and both of her aunts.

The trouble was, what she witnessed didn't help dilute any of her attraction for him. Any of her rapidly growing feelings for him. Any of her desire for him.

So, as much as she loved and appreciated her family, Carly couldn't help counting the minutes until she and Bax could say good-night.

Of course, once they did she started to wonder how she was going to keep their time together from ending prematurely, but he took care of that when he pulled into the driveway at ten o'clock and said, "I haven't given you my present yet. How 'bout I bring that and a bottle of wine out to the cottage for a change so I'm the one who has to go home afterward?"

Carly laughed. "Oh, good. It's been such a long trek for me to get home those other times."

He just smiled, got out of the car and again came around for her.

Carly went ahead of him through the main house and out to the cottage, wanting to make sure her tiny, temporary lodgings were in order before he followed.

Luckily she didn't have much tidying up to do because he didn't give her ten minutes before he was knocking on the cottage door.

"Come on in," she called as she let a sense of decadence have its way with her and lit the room with only the three vanilla candles that decorated the center of the coffee table in front of the love seat that made up the biggest part of the living room section of the guest house.

Bax did as he was told, bringing with him a small, gaily wrapped package, a bottle of wine, two glasses…and bare feet—something Carly noticed right off the bat.

"New boots. They were killing me," he said when he caught the direction of her eyes. "Hope you don't mind."

Since she'd already shed her own single shoe she could hardly complain.

Not that she would have, anyway. She liked the relaxed, comfortable intimacy of his bare feet.

She liked it a lot.

But then there wasn't anything about Bax McDermot that she didn't like.

"I don't mind," she answered a little belatedly, going to the couch to sit and letting her crutches fall to the floor.

Bax joined her there, sitting at an angle that had him almost facing her.

"If you take this—" he held the gift out to her "—I can pour the wine."

Carly was only too happy to oblige, curious as to what he'd gotten her.

"Can I open it?" she asked as he did as he'd promised and filled both glasses with ruby-red liquid.

"Sure."

She was half expecting a pen-and-pencil set from the size and shape of the box and was pleasantly surprised to find a necklace inside.

"Oh, this is beautiful," she said, taking the silver lariat from its bed of velvet.

"I hope you like it."

"I love it," she said honestly.

She had on a denim sundress that was cut like a jumper though demurely enough not to need a shirt of any kind underneath it. Instead, the neckline split at the cleavage to expose a hint of white lace that gave the illusion that she had on a second layer when in fact she didn't. It left her throat and the upper portion of her chest bare—the perfect accommodation for the necklace.

She fastened it around her neck and then used her wineglass as a makeshift mirror.

"It really is beautiful," she reiterated.

"I'm glad you like it," Bax said, his eyes so intent on the necklace and the portion of her body where it rested that Carly could almost feel his gaze like a lover's caress.

He pulled his gaze upward with what appeared to be some difficulty then and Carly could have sworn her skin grew cooler with the loss.

"Happy birthday," he added.

"Thank you." She tried to turn down the wattage of her smile, but it wasn't easy when she was as thrilled as she was with her gift. "And thanks, too, for being so nice to all my family tonight at the party."

"I wasn't just being nice. I was havin' a great time. How often can a man have three gorgeous women catering to his every whim?"

"My mother stuffing you with enough food for three people, my aunt Gloria making you sing show tunes with her at the piano, and my aunt Tasha trying to drag you off to dance with her every two minutes? Anybody who'll go through all that as patiently as you did tonight can't be all bad."

Bax gave her the devilish grin. "Maybe not *all* bad. But a little. When it counts."

The innuendo in his voice went along with the grin and only increased the sensuality that had already begun to simmer in the air around them.

"You don't fool me, though," he said then.

"Was I trying to?"

"You make it sound as if you didn't get a big kick out of everything tonight and I know better."

Carly had the grace to laugh. "I like my aunts," she confessed.

"You like your aunts and your family and the folks at the boardinghouse and everybody we visited out on the farms and ranches the other afternoon, and the whole rest of this little town and what makes it tick. I'm startin' to think you're just one big fraud, pretendin' that you can't wait to get away from everything and everybody."

"I beg your pardon," she said in mock offense. "I don't speak badly of Elk Creek or anybody in it. I love Elk Creek. I just want to go out and see the rest of the world, too."

"Elk Creek is gonna miss you."

"Me? I don't know about that."

"I do. I think you're one of the town's sweethearts."

That made her blush.

"And I think you're gonna miss Elk Creek more than you think, too."

"Is that so?"

"It is," he said with confidence. "You may go out and find the Eiffel Tower and big-city lights and fancy restaurants and museums and galleries, but you won't find such clean air and so many folks thoughtful enough to bring food to the new town doc, or so many folks who look out for each other the way they do over at the boardinghouse—the way you do for them over at the boardinghouse. You won't find so many people wantin' to tell you those stories you love listenin' to or so many folks who care about you the way they do around here. And I'll tell you somethin' else, I'm gonna hate the thought of you bein' out in that big bad world by yourself with not nearly enough people recognizin' just what a gold mine of a woman you are.''

"A gold mine of a woman?'' she repeated with a laugh, not taking any of what he said too seriously because there was a note of levity to his tone the whole time he talked.

"An old-fashioned girl who has the biggest heart in town. Who's trusting and giving and sweet and—''

"Stop!'' she said with another blush and another laugh, this one embarrassed.

Bax looked deeply into her eyes, holding them with his sea-foam-green ones. "'Round here you're appreciated the way you should be. But out there…''

He made that sound as ominous as a melodramatic comic book and Carly laughed.

"Out there,'' she repeated in the same vein, "lurks ogres and monsters and evildoers of every ilk. Is that it?''

He grinned. "I was pouring it on a little thick, is that what you're tellin' me?''

"Just a little. But it's a refreshing change of pace. My mother and Deana usually opt for other tactics to convince me I shouldn't go.''

"Maybe because they don't want to lose you,''

he said then in a quiet voice that no longer joked or
teased. "And maybe I don't want to, either."

His eyes were still delving into hers and that, cou-
pled with words that had an impact of their own,
made Carly weak-kneed and lightheaded suddenly.

She set the glass on the coffee table and used the
motion as an excuse to tear her eyes away from Bax,
a little afraid of that impact and the weak-kneed,
light-headedness that went with it.

But when he put his wineglass on the table near
hers and turned back to her again, the spell was still
weaving itself around them and Carly lost herself in
that sight she was always starving for—the sharp
planes of that handsome face that drifted through her
dreams like an enticement.

"I have such a crush on you," he nearly whispered, making her smile once more. "A crush and
then some," he said more to himself than to her as
he leaned toward her and caught her lips with his in
a soft kiss that began and might have ended there
except that Carly met him halfway, kissed him back
and went on kissing him, indulging in that bliss she
never got enough of.

She'd been doing a lot of thinking about Bax
since the evening before. A lot of thinking. A lot of
yearning. A lot of wanting. A lot of wishing he was
with her. Alone with her. Holding her...

And right then she wasn't thinking about leaving
Elk Creek. She was only thinking about this man
who made her blood boil in her veins. Who had
carved out his own special spot in her every waking
thought. In her heart. This man who made every

nerve ending in her body sing and scream at once for more of him. More of his kisses. More of his Midas touch.

She was only thinking that when she was with him everything felt right. She felt complete in a way she'd never experienced before, with anyone else.

There were times, she decided, when it was good—no, necessary—to surrender to all those feelings, all those cravings and yearnings and desires. Just to surrender to the moment. To that one man...

And tonight felt as if that time had come.

So Carly went on kissing him, letting him kiss her with those supple, talented lips that began the magic. That slowly drew her to him, to their own private province where nothing mattered but the two of them, the feelings she had for him and the sensations that he was awakening within her with lips that were parted over hers and a tongue that had come to court, to play, to seduce.

His arms came around her, pulling her more closely to him, cradling her head in one hand as he deepened their kiss, pressing her backward.

She slid her arms around him, too, molding her palms to the honed, muscular mountains of his back, of his broad shoulders.

His mouth abandoned hers to kiss her eyes, her cheeks, her chin, her throat, and when he returned to her lips it was with a new intent, a more serious intent that sparked stronger passion, stronger desire in her.

So much passion, so much desire, that she ached for the touch of more than his lips. Ached to feel his hands not just bracing her. Ached to know more of the wonders of his touch than she had already.

Her back arched all on its own, relaying the needs of her flesh.

Bax got the message. He eased her farther back until she was resting flat against the sofa, with him beside her, his hands free to glide along the bare surface of her arms, her shoulders, her collarbone, worshiping the feel of her skin as if it were something he'd never experienced before, arousing every inch he touched and awakening an even greater need in her before answering that need with a course that reached its goal at her breast.

The dress had prohibited her wearing a bra and now she was glad for that, glad that there was only one layer shielding her from him. Because even that one layer seemed like too much.

Another arch of her back to meet his kneading hand let Bax know what she wanted. What she needed. And he finally slid that hand inside the denim.

Carly couldn't suppress the groan that escaped her throat at that first meeting of warm, masculine hand and soft, engorged flesh.

But it was a groan answered by Bax with one of his own as his mouth worked over hers in an open urgency and he explored the lush curve, the hardened nipple, the straining globe of her breast.

He found the zipper that closed her dress in back and slid it only far enough to slip the straps off her shoulders and lower the bodice. For a split second, cool air brushed across her bare skin and then he reclaimed her in a gentle, demanding, teasing, tormenting touch that drove her wild.

His mouth left hers once more, this time kissing and nibbling a path down the column of her neck to the hollow of her throat, and farther, finding just the beginning swell of her breast even as his fingers rolled the kerneled crest between tender, expert fingers.

And then he took that oh-so-aroused nipple into the hot moist velvet of his mouth, suckling, nipping, circling it with his tongue until Carly could barely breathe the pleasure was so great.

But she was still greedy for more. More of the feel of him. More of his body. More of him.

She tugged his shirt out of his jeans and made quick work of the snaps that held it closed, sliding it off him as soon as she was able.

His skin was hot and taut, satin over steel where muscles bulged and tensed with the power they contained.

But even that wasn't enough and so she let her fingers dive into the waistband at his spine, smoothing their way to his sides and even a little toward the front, giving as good as she got in teasing him, taunting him, even as she writhed beneath the glory of his mouth at her breast and cursed what remained of her clothes and his.

And then he stopped.

Slowly. Reluctantly. Kissing a path upward until he wasn't kissing her at all and instead looked down into her eyes, searching them.

"You didn't think this was a good idea last

night," he said in a ragged, raspy voice. "Has that changed?"

"I can't think of any better idea now," she barely managed to say as every cell in her body cried out for him.

"You're sure?"

"Oh, yes...oh, yes..." she breathed both in answer to his question and to the hand that had found its way under her skirt to brush feathery strokes on her thigh just above her knee.

"Then let's do it right."

Bax rolled away from her and got to his feet. He leaned over and blew out the candles, leaving the room dusted only in moonlight as he bent to pick up Carly, whisking her across the small room to her double bed.

But he didn't lie her on the mattress there. Instead, he set her carefully on her feet, kissing her again as he slid the zipper of her dress the rest of the way down and then pushed it and her panties to fall around her ankles.

Carly was only too glad to be rid of the barriers and hardly hesitated before reaching for the buttons of his jeans, unfastening them and giving that last article of clothing a shove that sent them to the floor, too, where Bax kicked them completely off.

It left him as naked as she was. Magnificently naked and so incredible to behold that that first sight of him, of his burgeoning desire for her, made her heart pound and her hands itch to touch him.

And touch him she did. That long, hard part of

him that proved he wanted her as much as she wanted him.

Again he swept her up into his arms, this time swinging her around to the bed, lying her there and joining her, his spectacular body following the length of hers, one thick thigh across her legs, holding her a willing prisoner as he recaptured her mouth with his.

He reached an arm over her to catch her hand, threading his fingers through hers, palm pressing palm as he raised her arm above her head.

Then he rose just enough to kiss the soft inside of her wrist, trailing those same downy kisses to the inner curve of her elbow, to the juncture where arm met body, to her shoulder, to the spot where her shoulder turned into her neck.

He rained kisses all the way down to her breast once more, to her nipple, all tight and yearning. To the delicate underside of her other breast. To her flat belly where his tongue traced her navel.

And then lower still...

Her eyes flew open in part surprise, part pleasure, as that warm, seeking mouth reached her. Her back came up off the bed and the "Ooh," that came through her lips came on a long, low, breathy sigh that was unlike anything she'd ever heard herself utter.

Then, when she could hardly breathe with wanting to feel their bodies united, he rose above her again in a glory of moonlit male beauty, finding his place between her legs, finding his home inside her.

Not all at once, but slowly, patiently, carefully, slipping into her until he'd achieved a perfect fit.

He moved only slightly at first. So slightly that it was just a pulse.

And then a second pulse.

And a third...

Carly flexed her hips into his, absorbing each movement no matter how slight, easing her own muscles in glorious answer to every withdrawal, waiting with growing anticipation for that next glorious plunge.

All the while she let her hands ride along on his back, filling themselves with massive shoulders, sliding down the expanse to his waist, reveling in the feel of that sexy derriere.

He quickened the pace then.

Faster.

Faster.

Diving into her farther and farther. Striving. Straining. Racing.

Passion grew apace with his speed and lit sparks at the very core of her.

Sparks that ignited into embers. Embers that flamed to life to blaze through her in white-hot flames that curled her spine completely off the mattress, that threatened to sear her with ecstasy so unbelievable, so incredible, so miraculous Carly wasn't sure she could endure it even as she cried out for more and tried to hang on to every exquisite moment. The same moment she felt Bax tense above her, within her. The same moment when she heard him call her name in a voice that sounded tortured and triumphant at once.

And then, too soon, the flames' blaze cooled to embers, to sparks. Until finally just pinpoints of light glittered all through her as both she and Bax calmed, quieted and relaxed so that every part of them melded together, entwined, as one.

There were no words to say in the midst of a union beyond measure. As hearts seemed to reach out to each other and join as completely as their bodies had.

Bax only pressed the gentlest of kisses to Carly's brow, held her tight and rolled them both to their sides where neither of them could resist the exhausted tug of sleep.

But even as Carly drifted off, wrapped in the cocoon of his body and feeling more wonderful than she'd ever felt in her life, she was a little afraid.

Afraid that the change to the grand scheme of things that she'd been so sure wouldn't happen might have just happened anyway...

Chapter Thirteen

Of all the times in his career that Bax had been roused out of a deep sleep in the middle of the night, never had he wanted to ignore his pager more than that night.

But the only people who had the number wouldn't use it unless it was an absolute necessity, so he had no choice but to slip his arms from around Carly where she slept so peacefully beside him, find his pager in his discarded pants pocket and then answer the 911 code.

Elk Creek's baby boom had struck. Three of the four babies due to increase the town's population decided to make their appearance all at once. And Bax could hardly complain about leaving Carly's bed when Tallie Shanahan—Tallie McDermot

VICTORIA PADE 213

now—had had only the second night of her marriage and what should have been her honeymoon ended abruptly, too.

When Bax got to the hospital portion of the medical facility just fifteen minutes after the call for help that Tallie had sent, he found his new sister-in-law with her hands more full than one midwife and a singular nurse's aide could handle. Ally and Jackson Heller, Ivey and Cully Culhane and Della and Yance Culhane were all about to welcome their new arrivals.

Luckily there were no complications, but both Bax and Tallie could have used roller skates to get around as the hours of labor and then the deliveries passed. And yet, even as busy as Bax was, Carly kept sneaking into his thoughts.

Carly, so warm and soft in that bed he'd left.

Carly in his arms. Carly beneath him, their bodies keeping perfect rhythm, fitting together as if they were two halves of a whole.

Carly calling his name at the height of passion.

Carly laughing, snuggling in beside him, every curve and hollow of her body molding to every hill and valley of his.

But it wasn't only their lovemaking and the afterglow that kept wafting through his mind.

There were also thoughts of Carly listening with such delight to the stories of the elderly Elk Creek residents.

Thoughts of Carly dancing with old Mr. Elton.

Of Carly bringing Mrs. Gordon brandy.

Of Carly with Evie Lee.

Of Carly with her family, humoring her quirky aunts, playing with her nephews, cradling her sister's new baby.

And then, too, there were thoughts of Carly pregnant and having a baby of Bax and Carly's own making....

The bottom line was that no matter how hard he tried throughout the rest of that night and into the early dawn, he couldn't stop thinking about her.

And even though he kept pushing the thoughts aside to deliver the laboring mothers—boys for Ally and Jackson, and for Ivey and Cully, and a girl for Della and Yance—the thoughts stayed with him. Got stronger. More insistent.

Until, on the way out of the medical building when everything was under control and mothers and babies were all resting comfortably, he finally gave in and explored those thoughts that had refused to stop.

Something had happened in the past twelve hours, he realized.

Something had happened during making love to Carly that had gelled his feelings for her, that had started him wanting more of her. More from her.

Because what he was thinking had gone beyond merely being unhappy with the idea of her leaving town. Beyond being loath to lose her.

It had gone to a strong, sharp image of the future. His future. With her in it.

Somehow, out of the blue, his thoughts had gone to a strong, sharp image of making Carly a part of his life.

A big part of it.

But that was exactly what he'd sworn not to do with any other woman for a long, long time to come. And certainly not with a woman who likely didn't want that kind of commitment. Not when it meant it would tie her down.

Tie her down...

That didn't sit well with him as he got into his car and headed for the McDermot ranch to pick up his daughter in the early morning sunshine. In fact, he hated the sound of it.

He didn't want to tie Carly down.

He just wanted her. In his future. In every day of it. In every night of it...

But how could he have one without causing the other? How could he have her in his future and not tie her down?

"Good luck coming up with a plan for that," he muttered to himself as he drove through the open countryside toward the ranch.

She'd seen right through his plan to point out the good things about the small town. She'd seen right through him, laughed as if he'd only been joking, and that had been that.

And now he wanted more than just for her to stick around.

Would she laugh at any hint of that, too? Would she even consider it?

And if she considered it, if she actually agreed to do it, then what? Would she feel *tied down* the way Alisha had? Would the same things happen?

"Then what would you have?" he asked himself.

But he knew the answer. He might have the kind of mess he'd had before. The kind of mess he was determined to spare Evie Lee.

His daughter was playing out in front of the ranch house when he pulled up the road that led to it and she stopped bouncing the ball she'd been dribbling to wave to him, her delight at seeing him written all over her cherubic face.

He couldn't do anything else that would hurt her, that was all there was to it. And he shouldn't even be thinking about it.

So again he pushed the thoughts out of his mind as he parked the car and got out, telling Evie Lee he was going inside to say hello to everybody before he took her home.

Yet once he'd done that, along with letting his family know the outcome of his and Tallie's night's work, once he and Evie Lee were in the car headed away from the ranch, those same persistent thoughts of Carly came right back.

And worse than before, they came back with a new edge to them. An edge that wouldn't allow him to so much as imagine a future without her when he tried.

"Is Carly home? Does she know about the babies?" Evie Lee asked then, interrupting his mental musings.

"She knew the babies were trying to be born, but not that they have been. And it's so early she might still be in bed."

In the bed he'd left her in. The bed where he'd

made love to her and sealed the fate that made it seem impossible for him to say goodbye to her.

The bed he wished he was sharing with her now. And forever...

"You like Carly a lot, don't you?" he heard himself ask his daughter before he was even sure he was going to broach the subject at all.

"Yep. A whole lot. We're friends."

"Mmm."

He hesitated to pursue what was on his mind, but in the end that, too, had a will of its own that he couldn't fight and he said, "Would you ever want to be more than friends with her?"

"You mean like *best* friends?"

"Or even more."

"What's more than best friends?"

"Like Alisha was," he said tentatively.

"Carly's not like Alisha," Evie Lee insisted defensively, wrinkling her perky little nose at the very idea. "Carly's nice. Even when you're not around. She's better than Alisha."

"Does that mean you wouldn't mind having Carly be, say, your stepmother? Or would you rather just keep her as your friend?"

He was walking on eggs, unsure if he should even be saying any of this to his daughter but concerned about so much as entertaining any of the thoughts that had been riddling him since leaving the guest cottage without first knowing how, exactly, Evie Lee felt about Carly.

Evie Lee gave his question serious consideration.

Serious enough to let Bax know she wasn't taking the suggestion lightly.

"Not that that's going to happen," he felt inclined to interject. "I'm just wondering what you thought about something like that."

"Isn't Carly goin' on her trip no more?"

"*Any*more," he corrected. "And yes, as far as I know, she is. I was just—"

"Pretend talkin'?" Evie Lee finished for him.

"Yeah. Pretend talking. What-iffing."

"Well, I didn't think I would ever want you to get married to no one else ever again."

"*Any*one else."

"*Any*one else. Ever again."

"I can understand that," he said.

"But I like Carly. And if she was my mom, she could comb my hair all the time and play with me and read to me and I guess that would be okay. 'Less she turned into like Alisha was. But I don't think that could happen because Carly's not the same as Alisha."

Except that she might feel as *tied down* as Alisha had felt.

Back to that.

But it wasn't something he could ignore and he knew it.

What if he somehow managed to convince Carly not to leave town, to become a part of his life, of Evie Lee's life, and she felt as tied down as Alisha had?

As Bax pulled into the driveway at home, he realized that even if Carly ever felt as tied down as

Alisha had, she wouldn't do what Alisha had done. Because Evie Lee was right, Carly was not like Alisha.

Carly was a natural nurturer. A natural mother. She mothered everyone. She'd been mothering Evie Lee already.

There was also none of Alisha's selfishness or self-centeredness in Carly, no matter what her former fiancé had tried to pin on her. Carly was generous and giving to a fault. She put other people ahead of herself, of her own needs and desires. Carly was definitely *not* Alisha.

But still, regardless of the fact that she wouldn't punish anyone else, the last thing Bax wanted was for her to *feel* tied down. Or not to do what she'd wanted to do since she was a child herself.

Maybe *he* was being the selfish one, he thought as he and Evie Lee got out of the car.

Maybe just thinking about trying to change Carly's mind about leaving was pure selfishness.

And that didn't sit any better with him than the thought that what he had in mind, what he wanted of her, might tie her down.

So what are you gonna do? he asked himself as he ushered his daughter into the house, feeling torn and tormented and at the same time elated to be even just that much nearer to where Carly was.

He could keep his mouth shut, he thought, answering his own question.

Although that meant watching her leave town—and maybe his life—forever.

But maybe that was the high road—not letting her

know how he felt about her. About her going. Making sure he didn't influence her or alter her plans or even make her think twice about leaving.

But high road or not, he didn't think he could actually do that when it meant most certainly losing her.

He couldn't let her just walk away without talking to her about it all. Because if he did, he knew he would spend the rest of his life wondering what might have happened if he had just been open and honest with her. If he'd just let her know he didn't want her to go.

Of course talking to her meant that he had to spill his guts. He had to lay everything out on the table.

Including his heart.

It meant that he'd be taking the risk that she didn't feel the same way he did. That she didn't feel the same way about him that he felt about her.

It meant he could still lose her.

But he didn't see any other way to deal with this.

So he had to take the risk.

He had to hang on to the hope that he wasn't making a mistake.

And he had to see if he could find a way that neither of them would come out on the losing end.

Brilliant sunshine flooded the guest cottage and woke Carly up early.

She opened her eyes to the empty side of the bed where Bax had been until the middle of the night when he'd been called away. She couldn't help smiling at the indentation in the pillow beside hers, smiling at the memory of soft kisses waking her to tell her he had to go deliver babies.

She longed for him to still be there. To be looking into his face at that moment. To be molding her naked body to his. To feel his arms come around her, pulling her close. To kiss his bewhiskered face. To make love again...

But since he wasn't there to do any of that, she had to content herself with just the pillow indentation.

She reached over and swept her fingertips along the curve, imagining it was warm from the heat of his body, resting her hand in the very center of it as if it connected her to him, willing him to come back to her bed.

But she could only stay there wishing for so long before she finally decided she had to get up, get dressed, get on with the day.

She made it as far as getting up, showering and dressing in her pink-and-white-striped sundress before a knock on the cottage door raised her hopes anew.

Cursing the crutches that kept her from running to answer the knock the way she wanted to, she called, "Come in," and then held her breath until the door opened and she could see who her visitor was.

She couldn't be sure if the sun really did seem brighter from behind Bax or if she just perceived it that way because she was so thrilled that it was him opening the door and coming in.

And again she had the urge to run, this time to

run to him, to throw her arms around his neck and kiss him and pick up where they'd left off the night before.

But instead she just said a cheery, "Hi," not wanting to seem as eager as she actually was.

"Mornin'," he answered in a sexy voice and with a lift to his eyebrow as he took in the sight of her from head to toe and seemed to like what he saw in her fresh-scrubbed appearance, her hair hanging loose around her shoulders.

It was only fair that he approved of the way she looked, Carly thought, since she was feasting on her first morning view of him, too.

He'd showered—she could tell because his hair was damp and the scent of soap and aftershave had come in with him. He wore a pair of faded jeans and a black Henley T-shirt that hugged every bulging muscle of his well-developed torso.

And all Carly could think was that there they both were, clean and put together, and maybe they could muss each other up all over again.

But Bax didn't seem inclined to do that as he remained standing just inside the door he'd closed behind him.

"Are there new babies?" Carly asked then.

"Three," he said, filling her in on the details.

When he'd finished outlining how busy he'd been while she'd gone on sleeping, she said, "Are you tuckered out?" almost hoping he was because she had visions of his napping for an hour or so in her bed and then crawling in with him.

"No, I'm not tired. I want to talk to you. Somethin' about all those babies got me to thinkin'."

"Births and deaths—I guess they'll do that to you," she said. But for some reason the tone of his voice, the look of solemnity on his handsome face, alarmed her slightly.

"It got me to thinkin'," he continued, "about you and me and the future and this traveling thing you're hell-bent on doing."

This traveling thing?

Carly didn't want to hear that the way she had. But to her it sounded so much like her former fiancé's references to her "silly little dreams" that she couldn't help being rubbed wrong by Bax's phrase.

"My plans, you mean," she corrected defensively.

"Your plans. They've been botherin' me all along. Since meetin' you and likin' you and…well, since comin' to feel about you the way I do."

He took a deep breath and sighed it out, switching his weight to one hip. "I just don't want you to go, Carly," he said matter-of-factly. "I want you here, in my life. I want you to be a part of my life. I want us to have a life together. I'm in love with you."

"Oh."

It was probably not the best thing to say. But he'd shocked her so thoroughly that it was the only thing that would come out of her mouth.

If he expected more, he didn't show it. He just went on. "I know it's quick, but there it is. I'm crazy, madly, wildly in love with you and I want you to stay here and marry me. I want you to be Evie Lee's stepmom. I want to have kids of our own and live here in Elk Creek until we're two shriveled-up old prunes who die holdin' hands on our porch swing sixty years from now.''

''We don't have a porch swing.'' Okay, that was worse than *oh*. But she was still so stunned by all he was saying that that, too, had just come out on its own.

But once more Bax continued with what he was saying as if what she'd said wasn't important yet. ''Here's what I've been thinkin'.''

He took a few steps toward her, but for some reason Carly didn't move to meet him halfway. She stayed glued to the spot, and she even discovered herself stiffening up a bit, although she wasn't sure why she did that, either.

Bax must have seen it because he stopped in his tracks, still a fair distance away when it seemed as if he'd intended to come closer.

But it didn't keep him from continuing with what he'd been about to say.

''I've been rackin' my brain with how things could work for us,'' he said then. ''What if I promise you at least one trip every year? Come hell or high water. Would that persuade you to stay?'' But he didn't stop long enough for her to answer. Instead, he forged ahead. ''I could get a doctor in here to sub for me and we'll go wherever you want to go. We'll see every single place you want to see. Together. I know it won't be exactly what you planned. It won't be all at once. You won't be living anywhere but here. But you'll see it all. And you'll have something to look forward to every year. Elk Creek really is a great little town and this way you wouldn't be leaving it behind, either. You'd still have your life here with the people you love, the people who love you...."

He was saying more in that vein, but Carly was feeling herself splitting into two parts even as he was laying it all out for her.

She knew where he was going with it and there was the part of her that was tempted by what he was proposing. Marrying him. Being a mother to Evie Lee. Seeing the world with Bax by her side. It was very enticing.

But there was the other part of her that kept thinking that she'd heard the promise he was making before. From Jeremy. A promise that had never been kept.

And if that promise hadn't been kept by Jeremy, how could it be kept by Bax of all people? Bax who was the new doctor.

She was a country doctor's daughter, after all. She knew better then anyone what that entailed. Emergencies and births and outbreaks and any number of obligations that had left her parents rarely leaving town for anything.

Carly felt her head shake before she even knew what she was going to say, stopping Bax's avalanche of words with the movement.

Then she heard, "It won't work," come out of her mouth.

"What won't work?"

"All of it. Any of it. Maybe you mean what you're saying—"

"*Maybe?* There's no maybe about it. What do you think? That I'm like that other guy? Just blowin' smoke to keep you around until you give up the idea of ever leaving at all?"

"I don't think you're being realistic. I think you're making a promise you can't keep even if you mean to."

"*Even if I mean to?* I'm giving you my word, Carly, that you'll see all the places you want to see. That I'll make sure of it. That I won't let anything stop us. That I'll make absolutely certain that contingencies are made for everything that might come up."

He sounded so sure of himself.

And it was tempting.

Oh, was it tempting.

To marry Bax. To have him all to herself forever and ever. To sleep every night in his arms the way she had the night before. To make love with him. To make a family with him. To see the world with him.

Carly couldn't have fantasized anything more appealing.

But she'd been blinded by a man once before. Blinded to the reality of things.

And even if Bax wasn't intentionally misleading her the way Jeremy had, even if he meant every word he said, she knew what was more likely to happen.

She knew that the promise would get broken. She

knew that the first thing to go by the wayside would be her trips.

And worse, she knew that she'd feel penned in just the way she had with Jeremy.

That she'd start to resent Bax, just the way she'd resented Jeremy.

That she'd start to feel as if her dreams really were silly.

That she'd feel diminished and petty and selfish— just the way she'd felt with Jeremy every time he'd come up with a reason, important or otherwise, why a trip had to be canceled or postponed.

And she just couldn't let any of that happen. Not again.

Her head shook of its own volition. "No. It just won't work," she said softly, hearing the pain in her own voice before she even felt it.

"It *will* work because I'll make it work," he insisted.

"I just don't think you can," she said firmly. "There will be medical problems you need to take care of and family matters that come up and kids to raise and problems and emergencies and—"

"And nothing that can't be handled. I'm telling you, I'll handle it, Carly. I won't let you take second place to anything."

"And then you'll be torn and harried and resentful and I'll feel guilty and selfish if I make you go through with the trips or penned in or tied down and resentful if I don't...." She put some effort into calming her voice because it had become as agitated as she envisioned them both feeling. "That's not good. It's no way to have a marriage. It'll chip away at us. At our relationship. And then where will we be? We'll be right where I ended up with Jeremy.

"It just won't work between us, Bax," she made herself say. "You've come here to be the town doctor. To put down roots. To raise Evie Lee where you can be a constant, handy part of her everyday life. And I'm packed and ready to leave the way I've planned since I was Evie Lee's age. That's how things are. You're ready to settle in. I'm ready to leave. And that's how things have to be. You won't be happy abandoning Elk Creek when it needs you—and it will *always* need you. You won't be happy leaving behind Evie Lee—or more kids—so we can traipse around the world. And if I stay, if I give up what I've always wanted, what I've always dreamed of and planned for, then I'll feel trapped...the way I felt before."

"Trapped," he repeated as if she'd hit him with the word.

"I'm sorry."

"And you're wrong. We both have family here to look after kids, and kids do fine being away from their parents for short spans. Or we'll take them with us. There's Tallie here to pick up the slack medically and other doctors who can come in temporarily. One of the great things about this place is that folks do for other folks. They help out. They care. So there are ways, Carly. Ways to make it all work. That other guy found ways to keep it *from* working. But I'm not that other guy any more than you're like my ex-wife. And I won't resent anything. I sure as hell won't make you feel penned in or tied down or trapped.''

She knew his intentions were good. But there was too much at stake. Too much that could tear them apart or make her feel bad about herself or make him feel things about her that she never wanted him to feel.

''I'm sorry,'' she said again. And then, with finality, ''It's just…it just won't work.''

''Only because you don't want it to work,'' he accused.

But there was no sense trying to deny that even though it wasn't true. No sense trying to make him understand what she believed would happen because she'd seen it all happen before.

So she just turned her back to Bax to let him know there was nothing more to say.

''Think about this, Carly. Think about what you're cutting off here.''

But she shook her head again. Stubbornly. Without looking at him. Because she was certain that she could see into the future where, if she agreed to what he wanted—to what a part of her wanted—they'd both have a life fraught with the kind of pitfalls she'd already encountered with Jeremy.

''Damn it, what do I have to do to prove to you that I can make this work? That I can give you what you want?''

''You can't,'' she barely whispered, so, so sorry that she believed it.

''You're wrong,'' he said once more.

But there didn't seem to be anything else for either of them to say, and so Carly just stayed where she was, her back to Bax, until she heard him leave.

And that was when the pain struck her like a body blow.

Chapter Fourteen

The rest of Sunday and all of Monday and Tuesday were the longest days of Carly's life. Maybe because she hadn't slept either Sunday or Monday night, so there didn't seem to be any break from one to the other, she thought as she sat soaking her foot in Deana's living room late Tuesday afternoon.

She'd moved out of the guest cottage within hours of her confrontation with Bax, telling Deana that the small house was making her claustrophobic when she'd asked to stay with her friend and neighbor.

But that was all she'd told Deana.

Carly wasn't sure why she hadn't confided in her friend. Certainly it was the first time in her life that she hadn't.

But she almost felt as if Deana wouldn't understand. Who *could* understand, after all? Carly wasn't altogether sure she understood herself. Not late at night, lying in the lonely twin-size bed in Deana's guest room, thinking about Bax and Evie Lee. Missing them both because she hadn't seen hide nor hair of either of them since Sunday morning. Wondering if they missed her. Wondering what Bax was doing. Wishing she were back where she'd been on Saturday night...

She'd spent a good part of those three days with her sprained ankle in a pan of water, trying to hurry the healing process so she could finally leave Elk Creek and put this whole thing behind her. That thought was the only thing that sustained her, that kept her from crying buckets of tears and being a complete mess.

But the truth was, even thoughts of traveling weren't helping a whole lot.

And that was an oddity she couldn't fathom.

No matter what bad or unpleasant or upsetting things had ever happened to her, daydreaming about seeing the world had always been her outlet. It had always had the power to comfort her, to soothe her. It had always allowed her an escape.

Until now.

Now not even that eased the heaviness in her heart. The constant knot in her stomach. The sleeplessness. The lack of energy or enthusiasm. The doldrums.

The thinking about Bax...

But still she kept telling herself that if she could just get out of town she'd be all right. Then she'd be able to put aside thoughts of him. Longings for him. Wanting him more than she wanted food or water.

Wouldn't she?

Of course she would.

Deana's doorbell rang just then, but it didn't have any effect on Carly. Not the way it had when she'd first moved in. She'd stopped perking up at the sound and waiting with baited breath as images of Bax being outside on the porch danced through her mind.

Now she knew better, knew that if he hadn't come around yet, he never would. So not so much as a glimmer of hope sprang to life at the sound.

Not that she *wanted* him to come around. Because she didn't. What good would it do anyway? Nothing had changed. Nothing could be changed by his coming around. In fact, she knew she'd only feel worse than she already did if she had to look even one more time at those chiseled features that turned her to mush, or at that body that singed her from the inside out with cravings. So it was good that Bax had never been on the ringing side of the door. When Deana came from the kitchen to answer the bell this time, Carly barely looked up from staring at the carpet.

Until Deana said, "Well, Evie Lee Lewis! Hello, there."

"Hi," Carly heard the little girl's response. "Is Carly here?"

"Why, yes, I believe she is. Would you like to come in and see for yourself?"

"I would," Evie Lee confirmed just before Deana pushed open the screen door and in came the little girl who was almost as much a feast for Carly's eyes as Bax would have been.

"There you are!" Evie Lee said as she bopped into Deana's living room in her bright-red overall shorts and white T-shirt, spotting Carly on the couch.

"Hi," Carly answered, fighting the unexpected wash of tears in her eyes and wondering what had gotten into her.

"I'm not s'pose to be here botherin' you but I was thinkin' and thinkin' 'bout you and so I came to see you. But don't tell my dad 'cuz he said he know'd you were over here 'cuz he saw'd you but that I wasn't s'pose to bother you."

"You're not a bother. You're never a bother," Carly was quick to assure, knowing she sounded starved for the child's company but unable to hide what she was feeling.

"Maybe I could get us some lemonade—how would that be?" Deana offered.

"I like lemonade," Evie Lee agreed. "And cookies, too. I like cookies, too."

Deana laughed. "I'll see if I can round up some of those, too."

Evie Lee crossed to the sofa and sat beside Carly. "Is your foot still hurt?"

"I'm afraid so. It's getting better, though."

Deana must have let her dog Sam in the back door then because the schnauzer came running into the living room barking his head off at Evie Lee as he did.

"He won't hurt you," Carly said, trying to quiet the dog.

"I know. I play with him through the fence in back sometimes when he's outside when I'm outside."

The dog finally stopped barking when Evie Lee petted him.

"He's a nice dog," Evie Lee decreed. "Kinda like the kittens at the ranch only louder."

"He does tricks," Carly said. "Do you want to see them?"

"Yeah!"

Carly put Sam through his paces, making him sit up and shake hands and roll over and play dead. Then she said, "Say 'please,' Sam. Say 'please.'"

Sam complied with a staccato yap.

"Oh, that's so cute! Now make him say 'Evie Lee Lewis!'"

Carly laughed and teared up again for no reason she could fathom, aching to wrap her arms around the adorable little girl and hang on tight.

"'Please' is all Sam can say," Deana informed as she rejoined them with a tray holding three glasses of lemonade and a plate of cookies.

Sam lost interest in anything but the cookies when Deana set the tray on the coffee table and Evie Lee knelt down on the floor nearby to have a closer look herself.

When she'd chosen a vanilla wafer and taken a sip of her lemonade, the little girl said, "This is just like a tea party." Then, to Carly she said, "Did you ask Deana 'bout French-braiding my hair yet?"

Carly was more in control of herself again and laughed once more at the child she took such delight in. "Not yet," she answered before explaining to Deana. "I told Evie Lee that when I'm gone you might braid her hair for her for special occasions."

"Sure, I'd be happy to," Deana said. "Want me to do it now?"

"Yeah! That would be good 'cuz I'm goin' out to stay at the ranch tonight and then I'll look pretty."

"I'll get a brush and a rubber band," Deana said, heading for the bathroom.

"You're going to spend the night at the ranch?" Carly asked Evie Lee, then hating herself for being so curious about why Bax would be sending her to the ranch. But she couldn't keep herself from remembering much too vividly what they'd done together the last time Evie Lee had been away on a sleep-over, and that curiosity about what he had planned without her was unbearable.

"I'm goin' to spend a whole while with them. And we're gonna have a barbecue and I can swim in the pool and play with the kittens and everything."

"Your dad must be real busy," Carly fished.

"He's pretty busy, all right."

"Seeing patients and getting into the routine of work, I imagine...." Carly said, subtly inviting Evie Lee to expand on the subject.

"And doin' a lot of stuff at home, too. On the telephone and stuff."

Deana came back with the hairbrush, a rubber band and a hand mirror then. She sat on the chair facing Carly and motioned for Evie Lee to kneel in front of her where the little girl would be in the right position to have her hair combed.

"I was at Miss Effie's some of the time yesterday and today," Evie Lee offered. "We had fun. We went to take walks and she bought me ice cream, but she doesn't know how to do French braids."

"Miss Effie's nice, though," Deana said.

Carly watched as her friend brushed and braided Evie Lee's hair, the two of them chattering away, and her heart hurt at the sight. She'd never felt so left out. So jealous. So much like someone on the outside looking in.

Maybe she really was selfish, the way Jeremy had accused, she thought. Because shouldn't she have been happy for Evie Lee? Deana could braid her hair the way she liked, and Miss Effie could take her for walks and buy her ice cream, and Evie Lee could have sleep-overs with the rest of her family at the ranch, and go on having an all-round wonderful time without having any need for Carly.

"There you go," Deana said when she'd finished, holding up the hand mirror for the little girl to see herself.

"Oh, that's pretty! Isn't it pretty, Carly?"

"Beautiful," Carly answered, hating that her voice cracked and that once again those strange tears filled her eyes. "You look beautiful, sweetie."

Evie Lee handed the mirror back to Deana. "I better go now before my dad knows I was here. But can I come back sometime?"

"Anytime," Deana answered. "But I think your dad will know you've been somewhere when you show up at home with a new hairdo."

"Oh."

The quandary on Evie Lee's face was precious, but even so Carly couldn't let her fret for long. "I think it'll be okay if you tell your dad you were here. I was glad to see you."

"And I didn't say nothin' bad, did I?"

"You didn't say anything bad at all. We just had a nice visit."

"Okay." Evie Lee went to the door by way of Sam, where he lay on the floor near the coffee table, petting him and telling him goodbye. Then to Carly and Deana she said, "See ya," and out she went while the two women watched her go.

Only when Evie Lee was outside and the door was closed behind her did Deana settle back in her seat to stare at Carly.

"All right. I've had it. What's going on with you?" she demanded.

"I don't know what you're talking about."

"Bull! I've been keeping my mouth shut, waiting for you to tell me, but I guess you're never going to unless I pry it out of you. But here you are, nearly crying at the sight of that little girl, and so now I'm prying. I know you didn't just feel cooped up in the cottage. I can see that something happened between

you and our new doctor over there and I want to
know what it was.''

Carly considered holding the line that nothing had
happened. But something about seeing Evie Lee had
raised too many things to the surface to go on not
confiding in her best friend.

So Carly let it all flood out. The whole story. Start
to finish. Omitting nothing. And finally letting Deana see just how much of a wreck she was.

When she'd finished, Deana merely shrugged and
said, ''You love him,'' as if that summed up everything and there was no doubt whatsoever that it was
true.

''I loved Jeremy, too,'' Carly countered.

''Not the same,'' Deana insisted. ''You may have
loved Jeremy, but you weren't *in* love with him. Not
the way you are with this guy. I think Jeremy was
just the dress rehearsal. But this is the real thing.
And you aren't going to be happy leaving the real
thing behind, no matter where you go or what you're
doing or seeing.''

For once there was nothing in Deana's tone that
hinted at ulterior motives of her own. Carly knew
her friend wasn't saying any of this because she
didn't want Carly to leave town. Deana was merely
stating the facts as she saw them.

''Jeremy played on your dreams of traveling to
get you interested in him,'' Deana continued. ''He
made himself sound like the perfect partner, and I
think that was the whole basis of your feelings for
him—he was more travel companion than life partner. So when you finally figured out that he wasn't

going to travel at all, there wasn't much left between you *except* feeling penned in. But from what you've said about Bax, from what I've seen when you're with him and what I saw today with Evie Lee, I'd say there's a lot more going on there. And you'd better think about it, Carly. Before you go running off. Unless I'm mistaken, I'd also say that even Elk Creek looks different to you with him around and you'll be making the biggest mistake of your life if you leave him and us behind now.''

Okay, so that last might have been somewhat on Deana's own behalf, but it didn't lessen the merit in what she'd said.

Before Carly could respond to any of it, though, the telephone rang and Deana went to the kitchen to answer it, leaving Carly alone to meditate on her friend's wisdom.

Uppermost in her mind was Deana's view that Carly hadn't been *in* love with Jeremy, that Carly had seen him more as a travel companion than as a life partner.

She'd never thought of it like that before, but as she considered it now, she realized her friend could be right.

Not that it had been intentional or conscious or even something Jeremy hadn't instigated and participated in himself. But yes, she and Jeremy had seemed to click when he'd begun talking about wanting to travel as much as she did. And yes, she'd counted on the two of them traveling together. And yes, only when she'd accepted that that wasn't ever going to happen had she started to resent him and feel penned in.

And no, she hadn't seen Bax in that light because she'd known from the get-go that he wasn't likely to do much traveling.

On the other hand, Bax as a life partner?

Carly could definitely see that.

And it was more appealing than anything she'd ever imagined with Jeremy.

But more than the difference between travel companion and life partner, was Deana right about the difference in how she felt about Bax? Carly asked herself. Had Jeremy only been the dress rehearsal for falling *in* love with Bax?

Carly thought about it. She examined her feelings then and now.

And she had to admit that her friend was right on that score, too. She'd loved Jeremy, but she hadn't been *in* love with him.

And she was *in* love with Bax.

Head over heels, deeply in love with him.

So in love with him that she wanted to be with him in a way she hadn't wanted to be with Jeremy— every minute of every day. Every minute of every night. Forever and ever. For the rest of her life.

So in love with him that she wasn't feeling the same interest, the same preoccupation, the same obsession she'd always felt with traveling, with seeing the world. Because suddenly none of that seemed worth anything if she didn't have Bax.

That realization rocked her to the core.

Never in her life had she felt that way about anyone. Never in her life had there been anyone or anything that had had the power to alter her dreams, her fantasies, of traveling.

Until now.

And now all she could think was that maybe she'd rather stretch out her travel plans to one trip a year with Bax than go anywhere for any amount of time without him.

Than risk losing him.

But what if those once-a-year trips didn't come to be? a little voice in the back of her mind asked. What if she stayed in Elk Creek, married Bax and never stepped foot out of the small town again?

That gave her pause.

And truthfully, she was afraid it would cause some anger, some resentment. Some of the feelings she'd ended up having with Jeremy.

But Bax isn't Jeremy, another voice in her head reminded her.

Jeremy had misled her.

Okay, he'd out-and-out lied to her. He'd *tried* to trap her.

But that wasn't Bax and she knew it. It wasn't something Bax would do. He didn't think her dreams were silly. He'd even agreed that the world was an amazing place and that there was nothing wrong with wanting to see it.

He'd also vowed that they'd have a trip a year, that he'd do whatever it took to accomplish it. And she believed him. She believed that he would work it out because that was the kind of man he was. Because he wasn't selfish the way Jeremy had been when it came right down to it. She'd seen Bax put his daughter first, seen him put his patients first— even before they were technically his patients—and she knew he'd meant it when he'd said he would never let her come second to anything.

Bax wasn't deceitful or manipulative the way Jeremy was, either. And he wasn't stuck in the kind of rut Jeremy had carved out for himself.

No, Bax would do everything he could to keep his promise and she knew it.

And if marrying him meant life here in Elk Creek?

Suddenly that seemed okay, too. Because yes, Deana was right again, and Bax being a part of the town did give it a new dimension for Carly. An added dimension that helped give everything more depth for her.

Not to mention that in his own way, he'd opened her eyes to things about Elk Creek that she'd always taken for granted, that she'd come to overlook— the goodness, the kindness, the thoughtfulness of the people; the closeness and caring they all shared; the strength of community. Things that she knew she'd never find in impersonal big cities.

And where else but Elk Creek could she and Bax spend every day never too far apart? Where else would they have so few distractions from each other? Where else could they raise their kids without ever having them far from sight?

Only in Elk Creek where Carly would be the person who braided Evie Lee's hair and taught her to bake cookies and took her to the park and watched her grow.

Only in Elk Creek where Bax could walk across the yard to have lunch—and maybe some other afternoon delights—with her.

Those were all things that had never seemed important until Bax and Evie Lee had come into her life. But they were things that held more appeal now than she could resist.

And when images of those things flitted through her mind, they left Carly certain that Deana had been right about one more thing. If she left Bax behind, if she left Evie Lee behind, if she left Elk Creek behind, it *would* be the biggest mistake of her life.

Carly pulled her foot out of the water it was soaking in then, deciding she'd wasted enough time, that she was going to dry off, bandage her ankle, get onto those crutches, hobble-march next door and tell Bax she loved him. That she loved Evie Lee. That she wanted to marry him. To live her life with him in Elk Creek. To see the world one trip at a time with him.

But she only got as far as bandaging her foot before the sound of several voices came from outside just as the doorbell rang again.

"I'll get it," she called to wherever Deana was since her friend hadn't returned from answering the phone.

Carly got up onto her crutches and went to the door, curious about the sounds coming from outside still and wondering if Evie Lee had collected a whole group of friends to bring back with her.

But when Carly opened the front door it wasn't to a bunch of children. It was to a contingent of adults. Her mother, her sister, her brother-in-law, her aunts, Miss Effie and Miss Lurlene and Mrs. Gordon and Mr. Elton, some of the Hellers and the Culhanes and a slew of other family and friends.

"Is this a lynch mob?" Carly joked, uncertain what was going on.

Then Deana came from somewhere else in the house, carrying Carly's packed bags just as Carly's brother-in-law and one of her cousins swept her up into a chair made of their clasped hands and deposited her in a wheelbarrow.

"The train's waiting and you're finally getting out of here!" Hope announced.

"Oh, no, I can't—"

"People more handicapped than you travel. You're doing fine enough on your crutches to get around and we're making sure no more of your trips get canceled," her mother added.

"No, you don't understand," Carly tried again.

But to no avail.

The men took her suitcases from Deana and Deana picked up the crutches that had fallen when Carly had been relocated to the wheelbarrow. All of a sudden everyone was in motion—including her—as the lot of them headed for Center Street, everyone talking at once about sending postcards and Paris and missing her and not worrying about anything and on and on as Carly kept trying to tell them to stop.

The thought of all her friends and family getting

together to whisk her away to the train station so she could finally have her dream was so sweet and funny and kind and thoughtful that it only made her want to stay in Elk Creek all the more. But no one was listening to her protests. Not even Deana who'd been instrumental in convincing her to choose Bax over leaving.

Instead they wheeled her down Center Street, gaining more and more people who cheered her on and only made the noise more impossible to be heard over, forming an impromptu parade past Kansas Heller's general store, past Margie Wilson's café, past all the other shops and businesses, past Linc Heller's Buckin' Bronco honky-tonk, all the way to the train station....

Where Bax McDermot was leaning against one of the posts that held up the roof over the platform beside the old-fashioned yellow-and-white station house.

His arms were crossed over his chest. His weight was all on one hip. And he was smiling a Cheshire cat smile as Carly was pulled from the wheelbarrow to be carried up the platform steps to him.

"Bax?" she said almost as if she didn't recognize him.

"I told you I'd do what I had to do to get you on your trips. And I'm provin' it," he shouted over the din.

"But—"

"But nothin'."

"You don't understand," she said over the cheers

as he pushed off the pole and picked her up into his arms.

"You'll have all the time you need later on to say whatever it is you want to say," he told her, carrying her to the three-car train waiting on the tracks behind them. "Now wave to everybody and tell them goodbye," he instructed.

"No! I don't want to go without you!" she said instead, panicking at the thought.

Bax just laughed. "Good thing...because you aren't. Now wave and say goodbye," he repeated.

Still unsure of what was happening, Carly did as she was told, waving over his shoulder as he climbed the stairs to a passenger car.

And then they were in a private compartment, away from some of the commotion still going on outside.

Bax set her on the double bed pulled down from a side wall of the compartment and stepped back, hands on his hips, staring down at her.

"Say you'll marry me," he commanded. "That we can have the honeymoon first and the wedding as soon as we get back."

Carly laughed, hardly believing what she was hearing. "It's a little unconventional, but yes, I'll marry you after we have our honeymoon. I was going to tell you that anyway—"

He cut off her words with a hand raised palm-outward, stepped from the compartment to the entrance steps again and called, "It's okay, she said yes. The wedding's on for when we get home."

Another cheer went up from the crowd, making

Carly laugh once more even as tears of joy filled her eyes.

But she'd blinked them away by the time Bax returned to close and lock the compartment door behind him and fall against it as if blocking any escape.

"Now, what was it you were tryin' to say?" he asked as the first turns of the train's wheels set them into motion.

"I was trying to say that I love you and I'd made up my mind to marry you and stay in Elk Creek—except for those once-a-year trips you promised me. You didn't have to prove you were good to your word. I believed you."

"Not before you didn't."

"Let's just say it took a little thinking out to get me there."

Bax pushed off the door and came to stand in front of her. He pulled her to her feet while still bearing most of her weight so she could balance on her good foot, holding her braced with his arms around her waist.

"Are you tellin' me I did all this for nothin'?"

She laughed once more. "Basically. But it was pretty impressive."

"Damn right it was."

"Where did this train come from, anyway? This isn't the time of day it hits town and this isn't the same train."

"I have connections with the railroad from years of my family moving cattle this way."

"And where are we going?"

"Denver first. Then Paris. We have ten days."

"Ten days that Evie Lee is spending at the ranch," Carly guessed, remembering what the little girl had told her earlier.

"And ten days that a friend of mine is comin' to town to take care of the medical side of things while Tallie and Ry go off on their honeymoon, too. I told you arrangements could always be made." His expression turned more serious then as he looked down into her eyes with those glorious sea-green ones of his. "I love you, Carly. I'll never let you feel penned in or tied down or trapped. And if you ever have even an inkling of any of that, all you have to do is let me know and we'll be on the next train out of town, headed for wherever you want to go."

But standing there in the circle of his arms, Carly couldn't imagine ever feeling anything but as wonderful as she felt at that moment.

"I love you, too," she said. "And even before you had me kidnapped I'd made up my mind that I wanted to be with you and Evie Lee in Elk Creek. That I didn't want to be anywhere that you weren't with me."

His supple mouth stretched into a slow grin just before he kissed her, a kiss that was soft and warm at first but rapidly turned deeper, branding her as his.

He picked her up into his arms once more, laying her on the bed and coming to lie beside her, kissing her again, this time with a flash flood of passion that Carly was only too eager to answer.

He undressed her and she undressed him, all in a

flurry of anxious fingers. Then hands began to explore, to find and stake claim with a new abandon born of the knowledge that they truly did belong to each other.

And as if their first lovemaking had only been the hors d'oeuvre, they feasted this time. Savoring every kiss, every touch, every caress, every inch of naked, aroused flesh until neither of them could wait any longer and Bax slipped inside her to take her to the limits of ecstasy where they clung together as they peaked at once, reaching the pinnacle that stamped and sealed their love, their commitment, and the life they would share.

And then they lay, still entwined, sated and blissful in the blush of lovemaking that Carly knew was really only the beginning of everything for them.

"I love you, Carly," Bax repeated.

"I love you, too."

"Will you marry me and be my wife and be Evie Lee's stepmom and mom to however many other kidlets we have and see the world with me, too?"

Carly smiled against his chest and yet again felt her eyes grow damp with happy tears. "That has to be the longest proposal in history."

"I wanted to make sure I covered everything. What's your answer—for the record?"

"Yes. My answer is yes, I will marry you and be your wife and Evie Lee's stepmom and mom to however many other kidlets we have and see the world with you."

"Then I can die a happy man."

"But not for sixty years—you promised me sixty years."

"At least," he whispered.

Carly felt him relax and slowly fall asleep as she settled in, comfortably molded to his side, the train bouncing along beneath them.

And somehow she knew in her heart that she would never feel any regrets for this, for changing her plans, for altering her dreams.

Because in Bax's arms was all the world she needed. All the world she would ever need.

And anything else would just be a bonus.

* * * * *

Don't miss Victoria Pade's next novel,
THE MARRIAGE BARGAIN, part of
MONTANA MAVERICKS:
WED IN WHITEHORN,
on sale September 2000.

If you enjoyed what you just read,
then we've got an offer you can't resist!

Take 2 bestselling love stories FREE!

Plus get a FREE surprise gift!

Clip this page and mail it to Silhouette Reader Service™

IN U.S.A.	IN CANADA
3010 Walden Ave.	P.O. Box 609
P.O. Box 1867	Fort Erie, Ontario
Buffalo, N.Y. 14240-1867	L2A 5X3

YES! Please send me 2 free Silhouette Special Edition® novels and my free surprise gift. Then send me 6 brand-new novels every month, which I will receive months before they're available in stores. In the U.S.A., bill me at the bargain price of $3.80 plus 25¢ delivery per book and applicable sales tax, if any*. In Canada, bill me at the bargain price of $4.21 plus 25¢ delivery per book and applicable taxes**. That's the complete price and a savings of at least 10% off the cover prices—what a great deal! I understand that accepting the 2 free books and gift places me under no obligation ever to buy any books. I can always return a shipment and cancel at any time. Even if I never buy another book from Silhouette, the 2 free books and gift are mine to keep forever. So why not take us up on our invitation. You'll be glad you did!

235 SEN C224
335 SEN C225

Name	(PLEASE PRINT)	
Address	Apt.#	
City	State/Prov.	Zip/Postal Code

* Terms and prices subject to change without notice. Sales tax applicable in N.Y.
** Canadian residents will be charged applicable provincial taxes and GST.
   All orders subject to approval. Offer limited to one per household.
   ® are registered trademarks of Harlequin Enterprises Limited.

SPED00   ©1998 Harlequin Enterprises Limited

Look who's celebrating our 20th Anniversary:

Celebrate
20
YEARS

"Let's raise a glass to Silhouette and all the great books and talented authors they've introduced over the past twenty years. May the *next* twenty be just as exciting and just as innovative!"

—*New York Times* bestselling author
Linda Lael Miller

"A visit to Silhouette is a guaranteed happy ending, a chance to touch magic for a little while.... I hope Silhouette goes on forever."

—International bestselling author
Marie Ferrarella

"Twenty years of laughter and love. It's not hard to imagine Silhouette Books celebrating twenty years of quality publishing, but it is hard to imagine a publishing world without it. Congratulations."

—International bestselling author
Emilie Richards

Silhouette ® SPECIAL EDITION ®

Visit us at www.romance.net

PS20SSEAQ1

SILHOUETTE'S 20ᵀᴴ ANNIVERSARY CONTEST
OFFICIAL RULES
NO PURCHASE NECESSARY TO ENTER

1. To enter, follow directions published in the offer to which you are responding. Contest begins 1/1/00 and ends on 8/24/00 (the "Promotion Period"). Method of entry may vary. Mailed entries must be postmarked by 8/24/00, and received by 8/31/00.

2. During the Promotion Period, the Contest may be presented via the Internet. Entry via the Internet may be restricted to residents of certain geographic areas that are disclosed on the Web site. To enter via the Internet, if you are a resident of a geographic area in which Internet entry is permissible, follow the directions displayed on-line, including typing your essay of 100 words or fewer telling us "Where In The World Your Love Will Come Alive." On-line entries must be received by 11:59 p.m. Eastern Standard time on 8/24/00. Limit one e-mail entry per person, household and e-mail address per day, per presentation. If you are a resident of a geographic area in which entry via the Internet is permissible, you may, in lieu of submitting an entry on-line, enter by mail, by hand-printing your name, address, telephone number and contest number/name on an 8"x 11" plain piece of paper and telling us in 100 words or fewer "Where In The World Your Love Will Come Alive," and mailing via first-class mail to: Silhouette 20ᵗʰ Anniversary Contest, (in the U.S.) P.O. Box 9069, Buffalo, NY 14269-9069; (In Canada) P.O. Box 637, Fort Erie, Ontario, Canada L2A 5X3. Limit one 8"x 11" mailed entry per person, household and e-mail address per day. On-line and/or 8"x 11" mailed entries received from persons residing in geographic areas in which Internet entry is not permissible will be disqualified. No liability is assumed for lost, late, incomplete, inaccurate, nondelivered or misdirected mail, or misdirected e-mail, for technical, hardware or software failures of any kind, lost or unavailable network connection, or failed, incomplete, garbled or delayed computer transmission or any human error which may occur in the receipt or processing of the entries in the contest.

3. Essays will be judged by a panel of members of the Silhouette editorial and marketing staff based on the following criteria:

   Sincerity (believability, credibility)—50%
   Originality (freshness, creativity)—30%
   Aptness (appropriateness to contest ideas)—20%

   Purchase or acceptance of a product offer does not improve your chances of winning. In the event of a tie, duplicate prizes will be awarded.

4. All entries become the property of Harlequin Enterprises Ltd., and will not be returned. Winner will be determined no later than 10/31/00 and will be notified by mail. Grand Prize winner will be required to sign and return Affidavit of Eligibility within 15 days of receipt of notification. Noncompliance within the time period may result in disqualification and an alternative winner may be selected. All municipal, provincial, federal, state and local laws and regulations apply. Contest open only to residents of the U.S. and Canada who are 18 years of age or older, and is void wherever prohibited by law. Internet entry is restricted solely to residents of those geographical areas in which Internet entry is permissible. Employees of Torstar Corp., their affiliates, agents and members of their immediate families are not eligible. Taxes on the prizes are the sole responsibility of winners. Entry and acceptance of any prize offered constitutes permission to use winner's name, photograph or other likeness for the purposes of advertising, trade and promotion on behalf of Torstar Corp. without further compensation to the winner, unless prohibited by law. Torstar Corp and D.L. Blair, Inc., their parents, affiliates and subsidiaries, are not responsible for errors in printing or electronic presentation of contest or entries. In the event of printing or other errors which may result in unintended prize values or duplication of prizes, all affected contest materials or entries shall be null and void. If for any reason the Internet portion of the contest is not capable of running as planned, including infection by computer virus, bugs, tampering, unauthorized intervention, fraud, technical failures, or any other causes beyond the control of Torstar Corp. which corrupt or affect the administration, secrecy, fairness, integrity or proper conduct of the contest, Torstar Corp. reserves the right, at its sole discretion, to disqualify any individual who tampers with the entry process and to cancel, terminate, modify or suspend the contest or the Internet portion thereof. In the event of a dispute regarding an on-line entry, the entry will be deemed submitted by the authorized holder of the e-mail account submitted at the time of entry. Authorized account holder is defined as the natural person who is assigned to an e-mail address by an Internet access provider, on-line service provider or other organization that is responsible for arranging e-mail address for the domain associated with the submitted e-mail address.

5. Prizes: Grand Prize—a $10,000 vacation to anywhere in the world. Travelers (at least one must be 18 years of age or older) or parent or guardian if one traveler is a minor, must sign and return a Release of Liability prior to departure. Travel must be completed by December 31, 2001, and is subject to space and accommodations availability. Two hundred (200) Second Prizes—a two-book limited edition autographed collector set from one of the Silhouette Anniversary authors: Nora Roberts, Diana Palmer, Linda Howard or Annette Broadrick (value $10.00 each set). All prizes are valued in U.S. dollars.

6. For a list of winners (available after 10/31/00), send a self-addressed, stamped envelope to: Harlequin Silhouette 20ᵗʰ Anniversary Winners, P.O. Box 4200, Blair, NE 68009-4200.

Contest sponsored by Torstar Corp., P.O. Box 9042, Buffalo, NY 14269-9042.

ENTER FOR A CHANCE TO WIN*

Silhouette's 20th Anniversary Contest

Tell Us Where in the World
You Would Like *Your* Love To Come Alive...
And We'll Send the Lucky Winner There!

Silhouette wants to take you wherever
your happy ending can come true.

Here's how to enter: Tell us, in 100 words or less,
where you want to go to make your love come alive!

In addition to the grand prize, there will be 200
runner-up prizes, collector's-edition book sets
autographed by one of the Silhouette anniversary
authors: **Nora Roberts, Diana Palmer,
Linda Howard** or **Annette Broadrick**.

DON'T MISS YOUR CHANCE TO WIN!
ENTER NOW! No Purchase Necessary

Silhouette®
Where love comes alive™

Name: _____

Address: _____

City: _____ State/Province: _____

Zip/Postal Code: _____

Mail to Harlequin Books: **In the U.S.:** P.O. Box 9069, Buffalo, NY
14269-9069; **In Canada:** P.O. Box 637, Fort Erie, Ontario, L4A 5X3

PS20CON_R